THE SKUNK CODE

D.R.SMITH

Chicken House

2 palmer street, frome, somerset BA11 1dS
www.doublecluck.com.

This book is for my parents, Jess and Harry,
who waited so long for me to write.

Text © D. R. Smith 2006

First published in Great Britain in 2006 by
The Chicken House
2 Palmer Street
Frome, Somerset BA11 1DS
United Kingdom
www.doublecluck.com

D. R. Smith has asserted his rights under the Copyright, Designs and Patents Act,
1988, to be identified as the author of this work.

Cover design by Radio
Designed and typeset by Dorchester Typesetting Group Ltd
Printed and bound in Great Britain

1 3 5 7 9 10 8 6 4 2

British Library Cataloguing in Publication data available.

10 digit ISBN 1 904442 50 1
13 digit ISBN 978 1904442 50 9

I would also like to take this opportunity
to thank my editor, Imogen Cooper,
for all her help in making
The Skunk Code what it is today.

From The Chicken House

Clever kids, magic tricks, and a villain to make your flesh creep! A real blast of an adventure. If this book doesn't make you want to be a MI21 secret agent, then you'd better go back to sleep right now!

So, there's this unbreakable code, right, and ...

Barry Cunningham
Publisher and Spy Seeker

CHAPTER 1

'Last chance, you squirming maggot!'

THERE MAY BE MANY THINGS WORSE THAN being dangled upside down on the end of a rope beneath an airborne helicopter, but right at this moment Samuel Piper couldn't think of one. Not one single thing! Being this terrified before lunch was not his idea of spending what should have been a quiet and relaxed Friday morning with nothing more than an English lesson to worry about.

What was he doing here? How did he get caught? There really must be something on that computer disc that he hadn't spotted.

Why is it that some days just don't go right from the moment you get up? You step out of bed, knocking half a glass of last night's orange juice over the sleeping cat; get clawed by the demented animal; fall backwards into the bedside cabinet, sending the lamp, books and a clock into orbit around your spinning head, and end up dangling underneath a black combat helicopter.

What is it with Fridays? thought Sam. *Why do Fridays hate me so much? The rest of the world loves a Friday because it's just hours away from the two best days of the week. Well, I hate them. Especially this one!*

The rotor blades of the helicopter pulsated through the wretched Friday sky as the machine moved closer to the speeding ground of fields and hedges. Mad Skunk Skuda (*pronounced Skooder*), villain – with bushy moustache and greasy black hair – stood at the open door with the rushing wind flapping and rippling his loose combat-style clothing. He stood there laughing, with one hand on the vertical rail at the side of the open door, a maniacal grin almost splitting his face. The index finger of his left hand was pushed firmly on to a button of the helicopter's winch control. Was he rescuing poor Sam? That would be the noble thing to do. But no! Our villain, our detestable Mad Skunk Skuda, had his finger on the button above which, in large luminous yellow letters, was painted the word DOWN.

'Down you go, Sam Piper. I've had enough of you and your silly games. First I'll deal with you and then I'll deal with your stupid little friend!'

Mad Skunk Skuda was pretty angry, but his crazy, chicken-like laugh cut through the pulsating air and echoed around the cabin. At last he had the opportunity to rid himself of this pesky lad, this horrid boy who just wouldn't do as he was asked. After all, Skuda only wanted a disc. Why would a boy risk everything to hold on to a computer disc that wasn't even his?

Mad Skunk Skuda's frustrated eyes peered over the edge, watching the descending cable that led to the trussed-up figure of Sam, who was flying through the air twenty metres below.

'I hate boys,' he shouted into the roaring air beneath. 'Particularly you! Give me the disc, you fruit cake!'

Sam could move neither arms nor legs and could only look down at the ground speeding past him, far below. Rope had been wrapped around his body many times, in great thick, tight, blood-stopping coils, then one end had been slipped over a large hook and attached to the helicopter winch. A heavy chain had been passed twice around his upper body and padlocked by his shoulder. As he flew upside down, the large padlock bashed against his cheek and chin.

Over the roar of the rushing wind and the throbbing rotor blades, Sam could just make out what Mad Skunk Skuda was shouting:

'Last chance, you squirming maggot! You've only got minutes left now. You'll never escape, and you know it! Tell me what I want to know! Where is it? Tell me! Tell me, you fool!'

Skuda's voice became lost to Sam as his pounding heart forced an even greater amount of blood to his head and ears, making clear thinking still more difficult. Fragments of the day's events flew through his mind. *Fruit juice; screeching cat; bedside table; lamp; clock; orbit; stars; helicopter; ropes; Mad Skunk Skuda; danger! What am I doing here?* thought Sam.

Mad Skunk Skuda laughed wildly as he turned and shouted forward into the cockpit.

'Trees ahead, Claudette! Time to go down! Nice, prickly, body-tearing trees!'

At the controls sat the elegantly beautiful Claudette, a woman whose looks turned heads wherever she went. It was impossible not to notice her. You just had to look. No one, young or old, male or female, could fail to glance in her direction. People would see the walk, the clothes, the confident poise, the immaculate hair. They would be drawn to her face; waiting to witness the blistering dazzle of her red and white smile. And then they would gaze into her fabulous green eyes. At this point, though they didn't know it, they were in mortal danger. For Claudette was an impressively powerful hypnotist. An intense, though fleeting stare could render her admirers completely at her mercy. All they had to do was to look into her eyes and they were hers, if she so wished.

■

Claudette could have been a world-famous model or film star, but she had more important things on her mind. There was a good reason why she was working with the disc-stealing Mad Skunk Skuda, piloting a helicopter and heading towards some distant wood. Claudette was ambitious and greedy. Skuda didn't know it yet, but Claudette was after his job.

'Going down, Skuda. Prickly trees coming up. Bearing 270 degrees.'

As the helicopter gave a sudden shallow dive Skuda turned to a seat at the back of the cabin. Here he stared into the frightened face of a young girl who was strapped to the seat with her feet bound. Skuda's smile slackened as he put on a more serious face and moved closer to the girl, blasting a lungful of his obnoxious breath into her face.

She wondered when he had last cleaned his teeth.

'Now then, my dear little Melanie: for the last time, where have you hidden that wretched disc?'

Melanie sat wide-eyed but said nothing.

'Don't you realize, you little creep, that this time I have won? I have beaten you and your friend. All those days chasing you around have finished. This is the end. Your friend is on the end of a very long dangly rope. He's upside down and heading for the trees. There is no escape this time. No more messing me about! It is finished! You will tell me exactly where the disc is. Or else when I pull the rope up there will be nothing left of your friend. No more Sam. No more adventures. It will all be over. All for the sake of a computer disc. Do you think his mother will thank you for keeping quiet? No, she'll hate you for ever and despise your whole family till the end of time!'

Mad Skunk Skuda leaned so far forward that their noses almost touched. 'Where is the disc, you worm!' he screamed, burping up last night's curry.

Melanie's wide, frightened eyes stared into his as the words of Uncle Jack drifted into her mind. *Under no circumstances allow Mad Skunk Skuda access to the computer disc. No matter what he says he is not to be given the disc. It could be disastrous if he opens any files. We will be there within twelve hours.* She shook her head slowly and kept her lips tightly shut. The Mad Skunk roared with frustration.

'Trees at 400 metres, Skuda,' called Claudette from the cockpit.

'Skim the boy across the top,' he instructed. 'Comb his hair for him. Give him a taste of what's really in store. He'll be bald before his father!'

Skuda then turned quickly towards Melanie. 'Did you hear that? 400 metres and closing!'

'300 metres.'

'300 metres,' repeated the wretched villain. 'Now, where is that disc?'

Outside, Sam swirled upside down in the speeding air: clouds and helicopter beyond his feet, green fields below his head. Every time he spun round he could see trees getting closer. He twisted his head to look towards the helicopter, checking that Skuda was not in the open doorway. He could hear him shouting at Mel.

'200 metres, you silly girl! Tell me where the disc is and I'll pull him up! Don't you like your friend any more? What's the matter with you? Why are girls so stupid?'

'Pardon, Skuda?' shouted Claudette

'Sorry, Claudette. I mean, why, Mel, are you so stupid?'

By now, Sam had slipped a small key from under his tongue and had clenched it firmly between his strong front teeth. Once again he checked that Mad Skunk Skuda was not looking down at him. Then, with surprising skill and ease, he managed to insert the key into the padlock banging against his shoulder.

'100 metres! Hurry up! Do you really want your friend to die?' roared Skuda, now red-faced and agitated, sweat trickling down from his greasy hairline. Mel was also perspiring now, she was worrying that she might not be doing the right thing. Was Sam all right? Should she save him by promising to hand over the disc? She tried to calm down a little and concentrate on her breathing. *Everything will be fine*, she thought. *He will escape. Sam has escaped many times in the past. Come on, Sam, you can do it!*

Sam was about to be skimmed across the top of the wood. His heart pounded louder in his ears and smacked against his chest as the bright-green leaves became a roaring, speeding blur, just centimetres from the top of his head. Still clasping the key firmly in his teeth he jerked his head against the padlock in an effort to open it. At that moment a small cluster of leaves, higher than the others, whipped into his face and chest and sent the key spinning from his teeth. *No! No! I need that!* thought Sam. The key glistened and spun in the sunlight, sailing away from him in a golden arc until it was lost in a distant part of the tree canopy. But just at that moment, the padlock cracked into his cheek with a different sound. It was open! The padlock was open! Sam turned his head as far as he could and caught the lock between his teeth. He pulled and twisted and finally managed to unclip the padlock and drop it into the passing trees.

'Skuda, we've cleared the wood now,' said Claudette. 'We've skimmed him over the top: brushed his hair for him, poor little chap!'

'Poor little chap! He's not a poor little chap. He's a menace to society. My society. Him and this, this *girl* are the bane of my life. Poor little chap, indeed. Well, he's going to be littler yet and he's going to have more than chapped lips!'

Skuda turned suddenly to Mel. 'We've cleared the trees. What do you think we're going to do now? Do you think we'll land and buy you a big, sloppy ice cream and then let you go home, skipping merrily through the fields?'

Mel gave the tiniest shake of her head. She knew exactly what the Mad Skunk would do next, but she didn't want to think about it. Although she wanted to burst inside she knew she must appear as calm as possible. She wouldn't let him see even one tear run down her cheek.

'Well then, what am I going to do if you don't tell me where that flamin' disc is, eh?' he roared, heaving his smelly breath at Mel like some revolting smokeless dragon. She flinched and jerked her head back, more from the odour than fear.

'You're going to turn the helicopter round,' she replied.

'And then what? Speak up, I can't hear you!'

'You're going to lower the cable.'

'Yes, yes . . . and then?'

'You're going to fly over the woods again,' Mel replied unhappily.

'Yes, that's right. Brilliant! And what will happen to Sam?'

Mel took her time before answering.

'He will hit the trees,' she whispered.

'See, you're not so stupid after all,' shouted Mad Skunk Skuda over the noise of the engine. 'And if poor old Sam *is* lost to the world by being ripped off the end of the rope, what have you still got to do?'

'I still have to tell you where the disc is.'

'And if you don't tell me?'

Quite calmly Mel replied, 'You will do the same to me.'

Mad Skunk Skuda stood up and moved towards the opening, placing his finger over the DOWN button.

'Right, Melanie, are you going to tell me where the wretched disc is?'

'No!'

'Oh, for goodness' sake! I've had enough. I've got other work to do. Back to the woods, Claudette. The lad's going down!'

'OK, Skuda,' yelled Claudette. 'Shame about the boy, though. He had a lovely smile!'

'Just concentrate on your job, will you. Lovely smile indeed! He won't be smiling in a minute. I'll wipe the smile off his face and everything else as well. And it will all be your fault, young lady,' he said, jabbing his finger angrily at Mel.

Outside, upside down and at over 60 miles per hour, Sam had finally managed to twist his arm into a very strange position and find one of the knots that bound his arms and chest so tightly. He was relieved to find it was a simple knot, one he had undone many times before. Quickly his nimble fingers worked the knot loose.

Eventually the chains around his body fell free and tumbled past his head. He pulled one arm through the ropes and began on another knot, to release his other arm. Finally, he reached up to start on the ropes tying his ankles to the hook. He was almost free, but he wasn't out of danger yet . . . the cable was still being lowered.

Mad Skunk Skuda stood at the doorway of the helicopter, leaning out to look towards the wood. He called back inside, 'Almost there now, Melanie. It's nearly all over. You've had this disc for five days and I'm getting tired of all your games. The disc is no good to you. You can't use it. It's not even yours. Just tell me where it is and we can pull Sam up, and no harm will come to the little fool!'

Meanwhile, Sam had managed to haul himself upright before releasing the last of the knots around his ankles. Ropes streamed and trailed behind him, some falling away into the fields far below. With one eye on Skuda's clothing flapping in the open doorway, and the other eye on the approaching wall of trees, Sam now had to attempt to climb the slippery, plastic-coated cable. Sam could climb ordinary rope with his eyes closed, but this was something different. It was one thing climbing ropes in the school hall, but in the buffeting wind of a rotor-blade down-blast, climbing a slippery cable would be almost impossible.

'Nearly there now, Melanie. There'll be a yank on the cable and then it will go loose. I don't think I can watch. It will be too gruesome!'

'Approaching woods, Skuda. Speed: 64 mph. Height: 50 metres. Cable length: 30 metres.'

Mad Skunk Skuda turned his head to peer down the cable at Sam. Mel was desperate to distract him. She knew that Sam would be trying to escape.

In a split second, she grabbed a full Coke can from the floor and concealed it behind her back just in case she needed a missile later on. Then she picked up an empty can from the seat next to her, took careful aim and threw it at the Mad Skunk.

Now, why Skuda hadn't fastened Mel's arms we shall never know, for he must have known about her fantastic throwing abilities. Nobody came anywhere near Mel in throwing competitions, and in darts Mel could score 180 with three throws, every time. Her throwing skill was famous, but unfortunately for Skuda he had forgotten about it, in his haste to do nasty things to Sam.

The empty can whizzed through the air and crashed into the Mad Skunk's left ear with a metallic crunch, just as he was about to look down the cable.

He turned round in the doorway, his face beetroot

red, steaming with anger. 'What did you do that for?' he demanded, as he rubbed his left ear and grabbed hold of the safety rail to steady himself.

'Let him go! Let Sam go! You horrible, vicious man!'

'Where's the disc, you horrible, vicious little girl?'

'Treetops in twenty seconds, Skuda,' Claudette informed them casually.

'I'm not telling you!' screamed Mel. She was feeling terrible inside but dared not show it. Desperate thoughts ran through her mind: *am I really doing the right thing? Shall I tell Skuda what he wants to know? What will Uncle Jack say if I give the disc away? What will Uncle Jack and all the others say if Sam is destroyed in a sea of whipping trees? It's only a grotty disc. We don't want it. It's no good to us. It only contains coded files. We don't understand what it's all about. All we know is that this lunatic, Mad Skunk Skuda, has been trying to capture us all week. It's obviously valuable to him but completely worthless to us. Let him have it! He can have the disc. I've got to save Sam. He's my best friend. I've got to do it!*

'Mr Skuda!'

'What?'

'I'll tell you where the disc is. Pull Sam up. Pull him up now! Please!'

CHAPTER 2

'He had such a lovely smile!'

THE HELICOPTER'S NOSE SUDDENLY ROSE in the air, almost knocking the Mad Skunk off balance. As he braced himself in the doorway, Mel noticed something move behind the villain's feet. There it was again. It was a hand, Sam's hand!

Now the top of Sam's fair head came into view. *He's done it! He's done it! I knew he would.* Sam's face appeared. He looked at Mel, and she willed herself not to smile. Although the helicopter was climbing, Sam was relatively safe now, standing on the helicopter's landing skids. He leaned down, out of view, and carefully began to haul up the cable.

'So, my sweet, tell me where my lovely disc is hiding. Right now,' demanded Skuda.

Mel looked straight at him. *Different game about to*

start, you Skunk, you rat. She smiled and then said calmly, 'Nah! I've changed my mind!'

Skuda gave a roar of frustration. 'Right, that's it!' he shouted. 'I obviously put the wrong person on the end of that hook. It should have been you! Sam would have told me where it was, for sure. He would have saved you. But you! You're nuts, little girl!'

He punched a button on the winch and shouted to his pilot, 'Down, Claudette. Back down to 50 metres. Down to the dark depths of Hell!'

From his hiding place outside the helicopter, Sam was hatching a plan. He could see that Skuda was wearing baggy combat trousers with turn-ups over his large thick boots. Holding the turn-ups in place were several short straps. *Perfect!* thought Sam. He raised himself up level with the back of Skuda's heels, slipped the hook on the end of the cable through the straps, and then crouched down, back out of sight.

'We're over the trees now, Skuda!' shouted Claudette from the cockpit.

'Did you hear that?' Mad Skunk Skuda asked Mel. 'Say goodbye to your friend, you'll not see him again!'

Thinking quickly, Sam started to shake the cable violently to make it look as if his trussed-up body was being buffeted in the treetops some 30 metres below. Skuda glanced at the cable in the winch.

'Oh, dear. Look at that! That poor little friend of

yours is being bashed to pieces. He's getting smaller all the time! Oh, I can't look! '

'And he had such a lovely smile,' chorused Claudette.

'Yes . . . lovely! Will you stop going on about it?'

Sam deliberately stopped rattling the cable.

'Oh, look! The rope's gone slack!' Skuda declared melodramatically. 'There's nothing left on the end. I wonder where he's gone. Poor little Sam! Claudette, bring this chopper to a standstill. We'll just hover while I see what's on the end of this cable. I warn you, it will not be a pretty sight. And then, you silly, silly girl, it will be your turn!'

Claudette slowed the helicopter. Mel tried desperately not to look at the cable hooked to Skuda's trousers, and Sam pulled himself under the machine as far as he dared, so that he wouldn't be seen too early.

The helicopter slowed to hovering speed. Skuda turned round to pull up the cable, but just as he reached the winch button he was thrown violently off balance from the tug of the cable on his ankles.

'What the . . . ?' Skuda toppled sideways, grabbing hold of the safety rail. Quick as a flash Mel seized the Coke can from behind her back and threw it with deadly accuracy at his hand. Skuda winced with pain and his fingers relaxed their grip a fraction.

Sam saw his chance; he grabbed hold of Skuda's ankle, and pulled. It was enough. Skuda fell forward, straight through the doorway and out into space, the cable streaming out behind him. To Sam he looked like an Olympic high-board diver sailing through the air with his feet nicely tucked together for maximum points from the judges. With a screaming curse of 'I'll get you for this!' the Mad Skunk disappeared through the canopy of trees in an explosion of breaking branches. Finally, the cable went slack as Skuda snapped off the end and crashed the last few metres to the ground.

Sam climbed into the cabin, crawled along the floor out of sight and began to untie the ropes around Mel's legs.

'You had me worried,' she whispered.

'I had me worried too! Good job you managed to slip me the key to the padlock before I went over the edge or I might not have done it at all. That was really close. I don't want one like that again.'

Mel smiled down at him. 'I knew you could do it. I just knew!'

'How did you get the key anyway?' asked Sam.

'Little bit of pickpocketing!' Mel answered, with a naughty laugh.

Sam finished untying the ropes and looked up. 'I've got a plan to get us out of here. Do you think you can do Skuda's voice? '

'Sure, no problem. It's very deep but I've been listening to it all day.'

Mel cupped her hands over her mouth and took a deep breath. 'Claudette!' she shouted in Skuda's voice.

Sam smiled, shaking his head. *How does she do that?* he thought. *No practising! She just does it!*

'Oh, there you are, Skuda,' replied Claudette. 'You had gone so quiet, I thought you'd fallen out of the helicopter!' she laughed.

'They've both gone, Claudette. There's nothing left on the end of the cable.' Mel sounded so convincing that Sam wanted to laugh.

'Oh, dear! She's no loss, but that poor little chap. He had such a . . . '

'Yes, yes, Claudette! He had a lovely smile.' Mel glanced over at Sam. He grinned back at her. 'Now let's land this chopper, Claudette, and go for a walk in the woods to see what's left of them.'

Sam grimaced and shook his head. It was a horrible thought and it could all have come true. He had escaped just in time and had his friend to thank for that.

'Oh, I couldn't do that, Skuda,' replied Claudette.

For a moment Mel threw Sam a worried look. Did Claudette know what was going on? Did she realize that Skuda had gone skydiving through the doorway? Bravely Mel continued in Skuda's voice.

'What? You can't land the chopper?'

'No . . . the walk in the woods! I'm not doing that. I'll stay in the helicopter. You can look for them by yourself. I'm going out tonight and it might put me off my dinner.'

'OK, just move forward to the fields and land carefully. I'll winch the cable up out of the trees.'

The helicopter moved forward. Sam crawled back to the opening and then stood up next to the winch control panel. Even if Claudette turned round now he didn't think he could be seen from the flight deck. In any case, Claudette would be concentrating on finding a safe place to land. Sam pressed the UP button and the winch whirred into action. Mel crawled across and held on to the rail. The helicopter soon cleared the trees and Sam signalled to Mel to say something.

'OK, Claudette, drop it down there,' she ordered, as a suitable landing space appeared beneath them.

The helicopter descended; the winch was still coming up. The ground, safety and freedom were getting closer all the time. Just a few more metres to go now.

'Come on, come on!' whispered Sam. All of a sudden the winch brought the hook and a trouser leg into view. Mel gasped, grabbed hold of Sam's arm and pointed.

'Oh, no! No, no, no!' whispered Sam, his heart in his mouth, fearing that Mad Skunk Skuda was about to reappear at the doorway.

As quickly as the thought had come it disappeared again. Their frightened faces turned to giggles as they realized that all there was on the end of the rope was Skuda's trousers, lost as he was catapulted into the tree-tops. They struggled to suppress their laughter as they imagined the trouserless Mad Skunk flying through the trees.

The ground was now only a few metres below them.

'Come on,' said Sam. 'Climb down on to the landing skids, and drop and run.'

'Right, let's get going!' replied Mel.

Sam, who was already halfway out of the doorway, couldn't believe it when he heard Mel shouting in Skuda's voice, 'Up, Claudette! Up quickly! The police are here!'

Laughing mischievously, Mel climbed down beside Sam. And as the helicopter changed direction and put its nose down for a quick getaway, the children jumped. Sprawled on the ground, they looked up to see the huge machine roar away over the fields, with Skuda's trousers flapping in the wind from the open doorway like some modern pirate's flag.

Sam stood up first and helped Mel to her feet.

'Come on, there's a village over this way. I noticed it when I was hanging upside down on the end of that rope. Great view from up there; I'll miss it!'

Mel thumped him on the arm.

'Sorry! Come on. Let's get ourselves home. I'm starving! And Mel ... '

'What?'

'Thanks!'

'Thanks for what?'

'For saving my life *and* not giving away the disc.'

They hugged each other with tears of relief in their eyes, then turned and ran across the fields, heading towards a village they could see in the distance. Tired though they were they ran most of the way, keeping their ears open for the sound of a returning helicopter.

As the children approached the village post office they heard the thunderous noise of an aeroplane. They stopped, turned and watched a Harrier GR7 bank around the closest fields. It slowed to a hover and seemed to watch them for a few moments, then, changing direction, it put its nose down, increased its thrust through the jet outlets and moved back in the direction it had come from, picking up speed as it went. Sam and Mel looked at each other and ran quickly into the post office to ask if they could make a phone call home.

Several miles away, flat on his back, amidst twigs, branches and a scattering of leaves and feathers, Mad Skunk Skuda, bruised, torn and battered, began to move.

CHAPTER 3

Missing information

AT THIS POINT YOU MAY FEEL THAT YOU need more information, as we appear to have arrived in the middle of this story, and have completely missed the beginning. However, it would be impossible to say what the beginning of this story was, as Mel and Sam have so many eventful days. Because, when Mel and Sam are not being chased around the country by lunatics after grotty computer discs, they often put on magic shows for their school, old folks' homes, hospitals and places like that. They are quite famous in their part of the country. Sam does a conjuring act, but is especially skilful at rope tricks, like lassoing Mel, or the headmaster, which is extremely popular. He is also an escapologist as, no doubt, many of you will have gathered.

Mel performs amazing throwing tricks. For

example, when they are performing outside she can make a Frisbee land on a tennis ball 20 metres away. She also has a special hunting boomerang, which she can throw at a tethered gas-filled balloon, burst it and have the boomerang return to her without having to take more than three steps. Sam and Mel even have their own coconut shy at which Mel demonstrates the skills that led to her being banned from all fête and fairground coconut shies for about 40 miles around.

However, in the 'Mel and Sam Spectacular Show' Mel also impersonates famous people. She has the ability to mimic almost anyone's voice – male or female, high pitched or deep, it really doesn't matter. She can impersonate members of the royal family, prime ministers, Members of Parliament, presidents, television personalities or just the teachers in her school (which has got her into trouble on a number of occasions!). She was even on a television talent show last year. You may have seen her. Melanie Eastwood is her name and she's sure to be on again in the future, most probably with Sam.

And where, you may ask, does Mad Skunk Skuda fit into all this? Well, have you ever heard of RapidoPost, the highly efficient and profitable parcel-delivery firm? Now, you didn't hear this from me, but RapidoPost is actually just a front for the Mad Skunk Empire, which makes its money by pirating CDs, designer clothing and perfumes, and importing and exporting illegal goods.

Mad Skunk Skuda is one of the top three Mad Skunks and completely without any scruples. He is out to get what he can for himself and for the Mad Skunk Empire. He is, without doubt, the most dangerous of all the Mad Skunks and is prepared to take enormous risks to achieve what he wants. Although he has been captured by the authorities on three occasions, he has never yet been imprisoned. Skuda is feared and respected. He will take on both difficult and easy missions. Two of the newer Mad Skunks made the mistake of complaining bitterly when Skuda claimed the task of retrieving a computer disc from two kids. Asking why he should have such an easy job when they had been told that he was quite capable of defeating the entire army of a Central American country single-handedly, one of the new boys was heard to say:

'Are you just going to take the easy jobs from now on and leave the more difficult stuff to us?'

Skuda was, of course, furious, but didn't show it. However, the two new Mad Skunks have not been seen since. No one but Skuda knows what happened to them.

So that's a little bit about the Mad Skunks and their empire, but I wonder whether you've heard of MI21?

You will know that all the major countries of the world have their own secret organizations, about which very little is known. You may have heard of the American FBI and CIA, the British MI5 and MI6 and the Russian KGB. There are many others, one of them being MI21 – The Ministry of Information for the 21st Century.

This organization began as a breakaway secret service working for the British. But with the collapse of communism in Europe and the reunification of Germany they became more of an internal European organization, helping to support the European Community in its efforts to stay together and to fight against smuggling, the slave trade, drugs trafficking and computer hacking.

Jack Sanders, MI21's European Director of Operations, is known by the name 'Uncle Jack' to most employees of MI21. Only the most senior members of the organization know his full name. However, he really is Mel's Uncle Jack as he is brother to Melanie's mother, Jeanette. Got it?

Now, through Uncle Jack, Mel and Sam have had very small tasks to carry out for MI21, but the delivery of the computer disc has been the most dangerous so far. Not that MI21 intended it to get that dangerous. Something went wrong. There is no way that Sam should have been trussed up and dangled on a rope from a helicopter, using all the tricks in the book to escape with his life. Something had gone very wrong and somebody was going to pay! And at the very centre of it all was a small computer disc. How did it become so important? Well . . .

CHAPTER 4

'We've got a Code Red'

LAST SUNDAY AFTERNOON MEL AND SAM were at Sam's house practising for their magic show when Mel's mobile phone rang. Mel stopped lassoing cones in the garden and went to answer it.

'Mel?'

'Yes.'

'Mel, this is Skydive, we've got a Code Red.'

Mel recognized the name of one of Uncle Jack's senior agents.

'There's been a chase on the edge of Whitewater and two of our cars have collided with one of theirs. We've got several casualties and only one of our agents, Vardoo, is mobile. He's chasing two Mad Skunks across town. They will probably get away with the prize, but there's a chance you may be able to help.

'I'm tracking Vardoo on our monitor. If you head towards the park, along Toadfield Avenue, there's a chance you may be able to help. Take something with you to distract the Skunks. Throw something or trip them up – do what you do best – but stay out of trouble or Uncle Jack will have my guts for garters.'

Mel put the phone down and filled Sam in.

'Wow, MI21 activity in Whitewater!' exclaimed Sam excitedly.

'Let's just be careful,' Mel replied. 'The Skunks might have guns.'

Mel and Sam packed four cricket balls and a coil of rope into a small backpack. Mel arranged her lasso over her shoulder and both of them dashed out into the street.

The moment they reached the entrance to Toadfield Avenue they heard the sound of running feet. They pulled back and peeped round the corner. They could see three men heading in their direction; two racing in front and another in pursuit, close behind.

Then, just as they were reaching the corner, the third man, who Mel and Sam assumed was the agent, Vardoo, misjudged his step as a small dog raced into the road in front of him, yapping wildly. His foot caught the edge of the pavement and he crashed into a lamppost, knocking himself out.

The two Skunks turned at the noise and came to

an abrupt halt.

'Thank goodness for that,' puffed one, as he took a computer disc out of his pocket and held it aloft. 'I couldn't have run much further. Now we can take this home. Skuda will be delighted!'

Mel took careful aim. A heavy weight thudded into the first Skunk's chest. He hadn't seen any movement from the side street, but he certainly felt the two cricket balls strike his chest and hand. The computer disc went flying. Then, before he realized what was happening, the second Mad Skunk found himself lassoed by Mel's cowboy rope. He was pulled sharply off balance and fell flat on his back on top of his mate.

Sam dashed forward and, keeping his eyes on the rapidly recovering Skunks, picked up the disc. He glanced anxiously at the unconscious MI21 agent, then shouted, 'Come on, Mel. We'll have to leave him. Time to go. Scatter!'

Immediately Mel and Sam took off in opposite directions, running for their lives, with the sounds of heavy footfalls close behind and Uncle Jack's voice in their heads:

'When pursued, never stay together if there's more than one enemy agent after you. Never run directly to any safe area and never, ever return home until you are absolutely sure that you have shaken them off. Find a hiding place where you can see, but not be seen. Stay

there. Watch and listen. Then, take the long way home, ever watchful.'

That was Rule 514 from the Agents' Handbook that Uncle Jack had given them when they had first started their MI21 activities. Between them they had memorized almost the whole book.

Mel and Sam are very fit, but grown men have long legs, so the children just had to keep avoiding the Skunks until they grew too weary to continue the chase.

Knowing the area helped a lot. They slipped under hedges and gates, jumped fences, ran between houses, behind sheds and under bridges. They stayed away from open spaces where they knew they could be caught, or even shot at, and worked by zigzagging through smaller areas, just managing to increase the distance between themselves and the clumping villains behind.

Eventually Mel and Sam found places to hide. They watched and waited and, two hours later, when they were convinced they had lost their followers, they each took a long route home to a late Sunday tea.

Of course, crawling under hedges and gates, and jumping fences, plays havoc with anyone's clothing, hands and knees, and therefore a mother's temper. So both children got into terrible trouble for not only being dreadfully late, but also for being filthy.

Even the most understanding parents can only take so much before they blow their tops. And, as Mel walked through her front door, her mother exploded: 'Look at the state of you, Melanie! For goodness' sake, this is a Sunday. Those are decent clothes you've got on, or they were. They'll be fit for nothing now! What on earth have you been doing? You were never like this, even as a three-year-old when you played with a bucket of mud and a bag of cement. Has Sam been with you? Is he in a state like this? Have you two been fighting? I'll have to phone his mother. No. Wait a minute. Wait a minute! It's Uncle Jack, isn't it? You're doing something for Uncle Jack. Oh, I know, I know, you can't say. Mustn't give any MI21 knowledge away! Silence means "Yes", Melanie. Right, I'm going to kill him! What's he got you doing this time? Not, saying, eh? Just in case I run outside and shout it out to a passing spy in a black suit, dark glasses and carrying a machinegun disguised as an umbrella. Why can't you two act like normal children? Oh, Melanie, just look at you! Go up and have a bath. Go on!'

Mothers can seem wicked sometimes, but they love you really.

Monday

On Monday evening Mel and Sam searched through the disc on Sam's computer. It had files under Word,

Excel and Publisher but very little made any sense. Some files were composed of short phrases, which looked like coded messages. Other files were a jumble of letters and symbols. Under a Word file they found a list of ten websites. They logged on to the Internet but after visiting five of the sites they gave up because they weren't interesting at all – one was even devoted to garden sheds! Another file contained two digital photos. One showed a dog sitting on a large upturned flowerpot, while the other displayed a couple, arms around each other, outside a cottage at sunset. In the distance was the silhouette of a column set on a rocky ridge.

They made a copy of the disc and Mel took it home to hide it under her secret floorboard panel.

Tuesday

During school on Tuesday they decided that if they hadn't heard from anybody in MI21 by 8.00 that night they would have to phone Uncle Jack to tell him what had happened. The only trouble was that Uncle Jack had said they were only to contact him directly if there was an emergency or they were in immediate danger.

'But Mel, we could be in danger, couldn't we? Those Skunks were after us because we had the disc. And they're professionals! I know we got away, but they have ways of tracking you down. They are probably searching for us right now! We must take the quickest way home and stay hidden for as long as it takes for an MI21 representative to get to us, though I really don't know why no one's been in touch yet.'

'Unless . . .'

'Unless what, Mel?'

'I've just thought. What if those men carried Vardoo off? Who would know we had the disc? No one from MI21, only Mad Skunks!'

Sam thought about this for a second. 'Oh, heck, you're right, Mel! Vardoo never saw us. He was knocked out cold. The only ones who know we've got it are those two crooks. This could be trouble.'

'We've got to get in touch with Uncle Jack tonight. The Skunks will be searching everywhere for us. I don't like this at all!'

'No, neither do I. But, we'll be fine, Mel. We've just got to be careful. So they don't find us.'

But the Skunks did: that very afternoon. Mel and Sam were spotted through 500x magnification binoculars from a nearby office block as they travelled home on the school bus. Within three minutes the bus was being followed, at a distance, by a red BMW. When the children stepped off the bus into the street, a cyclist followed them on the pavement for a while before attempting to pass them. He then clipped the gutter with his front wheel and crashed to the floor next to the two children. Sam and Mel, being kind and thoughtful children, helped him up, held his bike for him while he dusted himself down, and passed him his bag when he climbed back on to the saddle. The cyclist thanked them and cycled off down the road. For him the mission had been successful. Others, watching the scene from afar, could now withdraw out of sight to the darkened rear of a white Transit van, from which they could track the electronic signal, beaming out from the button-sized transmitter dropped into Mel's coat pocket by the cyclist. Within minutes the watchers would know where she lived.

Mad Skunks are professionals and their aim is to get what they want. So, at 2.00 the next morning, they moved silently and swiftly into Mel's house to retrieve the disc. The occupied rooms were quickly located and were then guarded by black-suited agents. The operation was carried out in darkness using high-intensity night-goggles. The electricity was switched off at the mains and the phone disconnected. Skunk members then systematically searched every room, moving every piece of furniture, lifting every rug, tearing carpets away from walls.

After twenty minutes it was clear that what they wanted had to be in the occupied bedrooms. A whispered voice drifted through the kitchen, 'Claudette, we need the aerosol spray. You go in.'

A dark figure, indistinguishable from the others in the house, moved up the stairs and nodded to the guard at the door of the front bedroom. He opened it silently and Claudette walked in.

CHAPTER 5

'Come quickly, and alone.'

Wednesday

HEN MEL CAME DOWN FOR BREAKFAST THE following morning she had a slightly fuzzy head and memories of some very peculiar dreams.

'Hi, honey,' said her mother from over by the sink. 'Gosh, you look as bad as I feel. I think I drank a funny glass of wine last night.'

Through blurred eyes, Mel could hardly see the dishevelled state of her mother, who stood with one hand on a tap, sporting hair that looked as if it had been in a three-round battle with Sam's crazy cat.

At this point, Mel went to get herself some breakfast and discovered three of the seven cereal boxes in the cupboard were upside down. Later, as her confused mind began to clear, she noticed that the contents of the fridge had been rearranged; photos on a unit were in a different order; two chairs had been swapped around in the front room; the order of books and CDs in her room had been altered, and there were dirty clothes in her drawers. But it would be much later in the day (12.15, to be exact – the time when she put her hand in her pocket and pulled out a peculiar little button-sized gadget) that she would suddenly realize what might have happened. However, by then it would be too late, because she would have led them straight to Sam's house and to the next stage in this escapade.

Mel's innocent walk towards Sam's home was monitored from a safe distance by the unseen Mad Skunks. Within minutes of the house being empty the Skunk team was swarming through it, combing through every square centimetre of floor and unit space in their efforts to find the missing computer disc; but, of course, they were wasting their time. Agents of MI21 – even young ones – are particularly clever at hiding objects. As the entire Mad Skunk organization was about to find out, these were not ordinary kids they were dealing with! They searched the house, and then returned everything back to what they thought was the original position. The only place they didn't look was in the hem of the long curtain in the front-room window.

* * *

At 12.15 Mel, who was just going out to the playground, pushed her hand into her pocket, hopefully searching for a lost sweet, but felt something unfamiliar and pulled out a strange little metal gadget. She glanced at it but then quickly put it back before anyone noticed and asked her what she had got. *Something's not right here*, she thought. *This is not mine. It's been put there, and it's a sensor of some kind.* She slipped into school, rummaged in her bag, came out with a pen and paper and then ran off to find Sam. He was with some friends but she carefully caught his eye and gave a surreptitious secret signal with two hands meaning, *Come quickly, and alone.*

As Sam moved over to her he noticed she was writing on a piece of paper. She signalled not to say a word. He moved closer and saw that she had written, *Say nothing, but look at this.* Mel produced the small metal object and slipped it into his hand. After looking at it he wrote back, *Where did you find it?* Quickly Mel scribbled, *In my coat pocket. I think it's been planted on me. Is it a microphone?*

Sam looked carefully at the object in his hands before saying out loud, 'No, Mel, I don't think it is. I've seen two like this before. It's a tracking device. They've found us! But I don't understand how any stranger got close enough to plant it on you.'

A thought suddenly shot into Mel's head. 'The man

on the bike, yesterday! He got close.'

'But that would mean they tracked you home last night. They could know where you live! They may even have been in your house last night. Or they might be there now!'

'I think they did come in last night. I noticed things had been moved slightly, this morning: cereal boxes, photos, nothing much, and me and Mum had awful headaches when we woke up!'

'Headaches? But that could mean you were drugged!'

'No, Sam, we would have heard them.'

'Not if they gassed the house.'

There was silence for a moment before Sam spoke again. 'They might have found the copy of the disc. You walked to my house wearing that coat, so they know where I live as well. There's been no one at home this morning, so they could have got in and searched everywhere. We've got to get back home as soon as possible, and this might just help us for a while,' Sam said, holding up the small metal transmitter. 'We've got to use it to give us some time.'

Why don't we catch a bus and leave the transmitter on board?'

'We can't just walk out of school. We've been in trouble for that before. I'll write a note and ask Charlie to give it to Mr Redshaw when she goes in.'

So they prepared a note and quietly passed it to their friend Charlie. On it was a message for the head-master. It read:

Sorry, Mister Redshaw, but we've got a Code Red. We have to go. You may have visitors looking for us. Don't believe them, whoever they are, whatever they say. Please verify this by phoning the following number: 0791 21 21 21. We may not be in tomorrow.
From
Melanie Eastwood and Samuel Piper

Sam and Mel thought that they were very lucky to have a tolerant headmaster. Mr Redshaw turned a blind eye to their escapades whenever they went out on special missions. Yet the school, Whitewater's Twisted Willow, had done very well out of these situations, and though he didn't understand that he was dealing with the Special Mission department of MI21, Mr Redshaw knew that by supporting the children in the past the school had received new library shelving, carpeting and computers. He would wait and see who these visitors were before phoning. He might get new chairs for the staff room this time!

Mel and Sam organized a pretend argument on the grass to distract the dinner ladies, then sneaked out through the side gate and ran around the corner to catch a bus in Woodlands. Luckily they didn't have to hide behind a wall too long before one arrived. They ran to the edge of the kerb and put their hands out, to stop the bus. The door opened, they stepped inside and Sam dropped the transmitter into the bin by the door.

'What's that?' asked the driver suspiciously.

'Chewing gum!' replied Sam.

'What are you doing out of school, anyway?'

'Going into town to do a transport survey. We're meeting the rest of the class there.'

'Yeah, right. I'll believe you, thousands wouldn't.'

Mel was about to answer back when Sam nudged her. There was no point in drawing attention to themselves. Instead Mel paid, smiled weakly and they both hurried to the back of the bus.

Five minutes later, and a couple of miles down the road, Sam rang the bell and the bus pulled over. 'Come on, let's go,' he said quietly, and together they jumped down on to the pavement.

Wednesday afternoon

While Mel and Sam took a circuitous route back to Sam's house to check whether the original computer disc had been found, Mad Skunk Skuda was organizing his unit to 'acquire' two police vehicles and several officers' uniforms. Then, just before the end of the dinner session, two police cars with sirens wailing screeched to a halt outside the school gates. Three officers got out of the cars and marched up to the reception area of the school. They demanded to see the headmaster at once, and when Mr Redshaw arrived they asked to be allowed to question the children from 18 Hillcrest Avenue and 35 Montrose Drive.

'Ah,' said Mr Redshaw with a smile. 'You will want to speak to Samuel Piper and Melanie Eastwood!' He was pleased that Charlie had just given him Mel and Sam's note, for now he knew what it meant.

'Yes. Samuel Piper and Melanie Eastwood. Write that down will you please, WPC Claudette,' said the sergeant, turning to the beautiful police officer at his side. Claudette gave Mr Redshaw a dazzling smile.

Without a thought he looked into her wonderful green eyes, failing to notice the hypnotic sparkle that hit him like a missile. Splat! There was a terrific crash as Mr Redshaw fainted and fell against the flower display next to the reception desk, soaking the visitors' book and shattering the deputy head's favourite vase.

When he came round a few minutes later, Mr Redshaw found his legs being held in the air by Miss Pinkley, one of the class teachers. She had taken a four-day course in first aid and was therefore entitled to do this to a headmaster – though in truth, nobody else had wanted to grab hold of his legs and hold them in the air, especially as they had seen what Mr Redshaw had stepped in as he walked through the school gates that morning.

'They've gone, Mr Redshaw,' Miss Pinkley informed him. 'They demanded to see Melanie and Samuel and then, after you had crashed into the flower display, another officer rushed in saying, "They're on the run. Moving into town from Woodlands!" Then they all dashed out of the school, jumped into their cars and sirened their way round the corner. What did the police want them for? And how did the police know that they were going into town? Are they in trouble? What have they done?'

Mr Redshaw tried to focus, but there was a mistiness forming around Miss Pinkley. He felt strange: Miss Pinkley looked almost attractive within her pink cloud. He only had time to announce that he had a headache coming on before he fainted again.

Sam and Mel eventually got safely into Sam's house after spending considerable time ensuring that the building was not being watched. But once inside Sam was suspicious. It wasn't just that the television was at a very slightly different angle in the living room, nor that his book of famous illusionists was upside down on the shelf. But when he opened his wardrobe and his demented cat shot out with hair sticking out at ninety degrees to its body, as if its tail had been stuck in a plug socket, Sam was instantly alert. Puffin did not get in there by himself and there was no way even Sam could have persuaded his claustrophobic cat to consider entering the wardrobe. Not even for a tin of salmon!

Sam suspected that out there, somewhere, there must be a Mad Skunk who had dared to push the crazy cat off its cushion on the settee. Puffin (don't ask how such a demented cat deserved such a cute name!) would have been quite happy for the whole Mad Skunk unit to ransack the entire house, street or town, and for them to carry on for a fortnight. But to be turfed off his cushion on the settee in the sun was enough to turn Puffin into a monster!

In fact, the Mad Skunk concerned will carry the scars on his hands, face, legs and stomach for the rest of his life. Puffin had become a whirling cloud of motion that clawed and spat its way all over the screaming intruder until eventually there was a desperate cry of *Claudette – spray!* And the ferocious animal collapsed in a heap on the floor. Then the unconscious cat was thrown into the wardrobe and the savaged and bleeding Mad Skunk was carried out to a waiting RapidoPost van.

So, just minutes after entering his home, Sam dropped to the floor of the front room. He crawled on his stomach to the window – just in case somebody was watching from a distance – and felt along the hem of the curtain until he located the disc. He turned, giving a thumbs-up sign to Mel, but said nothing, just in case the Skunks had planted listening devices. For according to the Agents' Handbook, Rule 354 section 3e:

'You may never see the microphone they've planted. It could have been there for years, or it might not be there at all!'

Sam indicated that they needed to leave as soon as possible. He picked up his mobile phone as they left for Mel's house.

'We'll have to phone Uncle Jack,' said Sam.

'But we can't use your phone for that!'

'Why not? We know the number.'

'Because you left it in the house. They might have tampered with it. They may be able to listen in, or trace and follow the call. We can't give them an MI21 phone number, can we?' asked Mel anxiously.

'I'm sure they didn't have time to fiddle with it.'

'Or they could have booby-trapped it. It might blow up!' Mel said, stopping Sam in his tracks. 'We'll use mine.'

She rummaged in her school bag for her phone, brought it out and dialled *0791 21 21 21*.

'Ministry of Information. How may I help you?' came the reply after just two rings.

'Security division, please.'

'There is a fault on the line,' came the coded

message from the receptionist. Without an up-to-date reply, Mel wouldn't be put through to the right department.

'The green ones are juicy.'

'Sorry, we no longer have green ones!'

Mel's coded answer was out of date. Now she was unlikely to get through to Uncle Jack. She wouldn't be able to tell him they were in a desperate state and needed help quickly. But then Mel thought she recognized the voice on the other end. There was hope yet. 'Is that Trudy? Trudy Blueshoes?'

'It may be. Though she may be off sick.'

'Trudy, this is Mel. Melanie Eastwood. We're in terrible trouble and I've just got to get a message to Uncle Jack.'

Over the phone Melanie could hear Trudy shouting, 'We've got a grounded bird here. Where's Jack?' And a distant reply of, 'He's out. Get him on the mobile, Trudy.'

'Mel, hang on a moment, I'm going to redirect you to a mobile. Best of luck, kid. The message here is you're about to 'ride a tiger'!'

'Trudy? What do you mean we're about to 'ride a tiger'? That doesn't sound too good! What do you know about this mission? Why am I a 'grounded bird'?'

'All the best, kid. Gotta go! See you at the other end.'

Mel turned to Sam. 'I haven't got a clue what she's

talking about.'

The line went dead for a moment and then they heard a familiar deep, rolling voice.

'Hello. This is Jack Sanders.'

'Uncle Jack! This is Mel.'

'Melanie! What's the problem? Is Sam with you?'

'Yes, he's here. We're OK, but things aren't going very well, Uncle Jack. We seem to be in a spot of trouble. We're being chased by some peculiar guys. They are really determined to get a disc we got from the Skunks chasing Vardoo.'

'You've still got it?'

'Yes, but . . . '

'Good, good. That really is very well done.'

'How did you know we've got the disc? We didn't think Vardoo had seen us.'

'He came to in time to see you running off. But he wasn't sure if the Skunks had taken it off you.'

'Uncle Jack, if you knew then why haven't you sent anybody to pick this disc up yet? We're in real danger here!'

'Yes, yes, we're aware of that. We sent two men in to take it from you last night, but they've completely disappeared. We fear the worst. We think the Skunks may have got to them already.'

'We need some help, Uncle Jack. We're not proper agents, are we? We can't fight off this gang on our own.'

'Have they found out where you live yet?'

'Yes, and they've been through every inch of both of our houses. They may even be bugged by now!'

'They've been inside? Ransacked the places?' asked Uncle Jack.

'No, very professional. Everything's been put back perfectly, but we can tell they've been in.'

'But you still have the disc?'

'Not on us, but it's safe.'

'Good. That's good, Mel. But listen, you can't go home again. You'll have to go to a safe house for the night. Go to Apple's. You'll be fine there. And we'll get to you by tomorrow. These Skunks must have the area sealed if we've had trouble getting our boys through.'

'Uncle Jack, can you phone the school and say we won't be in tomorrow?'

'No problem. I'm sure Mr Redshaw will be pleased to be compensated for your disappearance for a short while.'

'And will you get in touch with Mum, and Sam's parents, please?'

'I'll do that, Mel. Now then, you look after yourselves and somebody will be with you tomorrow. I'll spread the word that the two of you have gone up to Newcastle for a few days. I'll even leave an address. Hopefully, that will get these Skunks away from Whitewater. I know, I'll have your local paper print an article in tomorrow's paper about two missing children being found in Newcastle. They'll give your names and where you're supposed to be staying. That will send the Skunks off for a while.'

'Thanks, Uncle Jack!'

'Always a pleasure, Mel. Say "hi" to Sam for me. You're doing a great job, kids. Bye!' and the phone went dead again.

Mel put the mobile back in her bag. 'Come on, let's go home. We'll check that the back-up disc is still there and then we'll get a taxi and make our way to Apple's.'

'We can't take a taxi, can we? The Skunks may have all taxis and their call rooms covered.' —

'You're right. We'll take a bus so far, but then get off at different stops. It looks like we'll have to take rather a long walk across the fields.'

'It's better than risking it, Mel.'

In silence, they entered Mel's house. Things had certainly been moved, but Mel was glad to find that the intruders hadn't taken the ten-pound note sitting in a jar on one of her shelves. Nor had they found her special hiding place. She lifted the corner of the carpet in her bedroom, removed the small board, and put an arm around the corner and up behind the skirting board. Her copy of the disc was still there!

As the children left the house to catch a bus, they were completely unaware that a whole Skunk unit had just left Sam's house for the second time and were on their tracks. The Skunks were annoyed. Very annoyed. Though possibly not as annoyed as the bus driver who had been pulled over, his bus searched and all of his passengers questioned, or the two teenage passengers arrested on suspicion of being Samuel Piper and Melanie Eastwood, even though both of them were boys! The bus driver had to stand in horror as the police officers began to dismantle his vehicle, leaving piles of body plates and seats all over the pavement, until at last there was a cry of 'Aha! Here it is! It was in the bin.'

The mad-looking officer marched over to the driver, thrust the transmitter under his nose and snarled, 'I want to know how this got into your bin, and why you didn't tell us about it before.'

'I don't know anything about it!' the driver cried. 'I don't even know what it is.'

'Right, I'm gonna take you down the station and force you to remember how it got there. Somebody put it there. You must have seen somebody putting something in there!'

As he was being pushed towards a waiting police car the driver suddenly called out, 'Wait! Wait! I remember now. It was two kids! I asked them what they were doing out of school and I saw them put something in the bin. They said it was chewing gum!'

'Where were they going, these two kids?'

'Only into town to do a traffic survey. They could have walked. I don't know why they came on the bus.'

'To get rid of this, you fool! So we would chase you and not them. It's a transmitter, you idiot. Now we've lost them!'

'Well, they didn't go into town after all. Truanting, just as I thought. In my mirror I saw them cross over and walk down London Lake Road.'

Suddenly the driver was pushed aside, and all the officers piled into the two cars. 'Oi, what about all this?' he called out, pointing to the shattered debris around his bus.

Sergeant Skuda leaned out through a window and shouted back at him, 'I'm giving you one hour to put all your stuff back in that vehicle. If it's not done when I get back, I'm booking you for obstructing the highway, littering the pavement and endangering the lives of innocent pedestrians. Now get on with it, before I get really angry!'

As the children left Mel's house they could hear sirens in the distance. The sirens wailed and tyres screamed their way round corners in a desperate attempt to locate the children before they went to ground. But it was too late. Mel and Sam had run off in different directions to cach a bus for a quiet day at Apple's. Mad Skunk Skuda had lost them . . . for now!

CHAPTER 6

'So, that's how we got to the beginning.'

Thursday

THURSDAY DID PROVE TO BE A QUIET interlude. Mel and Sam tried to relax and attempted to forget the events of the previous day. It was a quiet day, but not an uneventful one.

Mel and Sam had met Apple before. She was quite old, even older than Uncle Jack, but she had once worked for both MI5 and MI21. Apple was a code name, created by some government genius who knew that she was a granny, and that her surname was Smith. She still works for secret government organizations, taking minor roles like looking after Skunk-tormented children on the run from an unknown fate.

The children were not allowed to leave Apple's home, but her garden was large and there was much to see and explore. Apple had free-range hens running everywhere and two goats in a small paddock, and they were enough to keep the children amused for hours. So it was with some disappointment that they received the phone call from Uncle Jack telling them that it was now safe to return home.

'What do you mean "It's safe to go home"?' Mel asked. 'It can't be. They were after us, just last night. They've been in our houses. They know where we live, they want that disc, and, anyway, I don't want to go home yet!'

'Mel, it's going to be all right. They really have gone. We fooled them into thinking you were up in Newcastle. The local radio there agreed to put out a report, and a local newspaper published a statement saying you had been found and were being housed in safe accommodation.'

'But what if some Skunks are still here in Whitewater, waiting for us?'

'They're not, Mel. We've had the place checked and we followed two Skunk cars out of the area. They've both gone up to Newcastle!'

'Uncle Jack?'

'Yes, Mel?

'If you've had men here in Whitewater, watching the Mad Skunks, why hasn't anyone been to collect the disc?'

'Ah . . . too dangerous to go to either of your houses in case they were being watched by the other side! We didn't want the Skunks to know we were around. They would get suspicious.'

'Well, they can get the disc off us this afternoon then, can't they? Or perhaps tonight? We want to get rid of it!'

'Not tonight. Tomorrow. We'll get in and retrieve it. Is it safe?'

'It's in Sam's house, hidden in the—'

'No, Mel. Don't tell me! Remember Rule 315: *Discuss nothing of secrecy over the phone.*' We'll be in touch tomorrow and pick it up after school tomorrow night.'

'But, Uncle Jack!'

'I've been in touch with your parents and a taxi will be with you in forty-five minutes. You will be dropped in Whitewater. Give my love to Apple.' The phone went dead.

Mel turned to Sam and explained that Uncle Jack thought it was safe for them to go home. The Mad Skunks had gone and the disc would be taken away tomorrow. But they both found it odd that Uncle Jack seemed so reluctant to pick up the disc. It just didn't add up.

'They've been saying that they'd pick it up all week. Something's not right.' Sam paced to the door and then came back, whispering, as if he didn't want Apple to hear. 'And another thing. When MI21 finally pick up this wretched disc, how will the Mad Skunks know that we haven't got it any more? Who will tell them? Do we put a sign on the door saying, "We haven't got it, so go away!" They're really going to believe that. Or will Uncle Jack announce it on the local radio and put it in the newspaper? I don't think they've thought this through at all!'

Suddenly, Apple appeared by the door. 'Come on, you two. You can have one more look for some eggs to take home for tea. Then it will be time for the taxi. And don't worry; everything will work out fine. Go home and have a good night's sleep!'

Friday
Early the next morning Sam, still more than half asleep, swung his legs out of bed. As his hand moved to turn on the light it brushed against an unfinished glass of last night's orange juice, which wobbled a bit before falling on its side. Unfortunately the contents cascaded over the comfortably sleeping Puffin.

In a split second the cat had taken off vertically, with legs scything the air like propeller blades. As it screeched and spat its way upwards, Sam, in an effort to escape, blundered into the bedside cabinet, sending the lamp, books and the clock into a tangled dance around his head, before they crashed around him.

Puffin, in an effort to escape, made an impressive, Olympic record leap to the safety of the top of a wardrobe. Sam raised himself to his feet and carefully made his way downstairs. He felt rather sick and had a dreadful headache.

In the kitchen, Sam's mum was in too much of a rush to get to work to have much sympathy for her son. She whirlwinded her way around the room, juggling cereal boxes, milk, spoons, sugar and tea, told him to have a nice day, said she was sorry he was feeling ill but hoped he wouldn't feel bad for too long, and then swept out through the door, only to return to kiss him on the head with 'Bye, pet.' Finally, she slammed the door with such force that every brain cell in Sam's head rattled like a china shop in an earthquake.

Just when he needed a friend, or the comforting arms of a parent, what did he get? A mother who had turned into a Force-12 hurricane, and a father who was worse than useless because he was away at a business conference in Manchester!

Sam walked to the telephone, dizzily holding on to the wall as he moved. He dialled Mel's number and her mother answered.

'Morning, Sam! How are you today?'

'The cat has attacked me, I feel sick, I've got a crashing headache, and it's only 8.30!'

'Oh dear, Sam, what a start to the day! I'll go and

get Mel for you. You are going to school, though, aren't you?'

'Yes, I'll be there. I'm not staying here with this cat. I think it's about to pounce again!'

Mel's mum laughed and soon his friend was on the phone.

'Bad day?' asked Mel, with a smile in her voice.

'The worst. This isn't a good start. I've got a terrible head. So I'm going to take the short cut to school today. I can't walk far, the way I'm feeling at the moment.'

'But Sam, we went that way on Wednesday. You know we shouldn't.'

'I know, but today I just want the quickest route to school. See you at the shop in fifteen minutes.'

As Sam walked to their meeting-place, Agents' Handbook Rule 511 didn't enter his befuddled brain. His head ached and he just wanted to get to school and sit down.

Mel was there outside the newsagent's. She was going to say *Sam, we shouldn't really go this way!* but when she saw how pale he looked she completely forgot her caution. Are you sure you want to go to school, Sam?'

'I'm sure. I'll feel better soon, and even school is more fun than spending any more time with our crazy cat!'

So they bought sweets, began to walk the same route to school as they had earlier that week, and totally forgot about the warnings in the Agents' Handbook. They crossed the road, walked over the green play area and strolled down the street. Then, as they came out of the alley next to the cinema, a stunningly beautiful woman stepped forward and sprayed the air around them with an aerosol can, shouting, 'Wasps! Wasps! Stand still children, I'll get them for you!'

The children started to panic, and that was the last thing they remembered as their hands went up to beat off the wasps that weren't there. Both of their brains seemed to melt as they collapsed to their knees, choking on the invisible gas.

It was only then that the words of the Agents' Handbook 511 came to them, clear and bright, before they sank into unconsciousness: *'When on a mission, whether large or small, never, never, ever follow the same route as the one you took the time before. Always change your route. Always! Confuse the enemy! That way they won't know where to ambush you.'*

Within seconds, a white van drew up beside the motionless bodies of the two children. Mad Skunk Skuda stepped out, and helped Claudette to haul Mel and Sam's limp forms into the open doors at the back.

A man, caught by surprise on his way to work, stood on the pavement watching them open-mouthed, knowing something was wrong, but not quite believing what he was seeing. As soon as the children were safely bundled inside Claudette gave him a blisteringly dazzling smile, took out her aerosol and sprayed the air around him. As the chemical cloud surrounded his body his eyes misted over, his knees bent and he slumped to the floor.

Then Claudette climbed up into the cab (unscathed by the contents of the aerosol can thanks to the inoculation she had given herself just twenty minutes before) and the van moved off into the traffic for a 30-minute journey towards a waiting helicopter and a death-defying dangle over the trees of Compton Wood.

So. That's how we got to the beginning.

CHAPTER 7

Bugs and a cascading briefcase

NOW WE CAN CARRY ON WITH THE STORY. The children have escaped from the helicopter and they're safe. For now. Saturday was a day of recovery. Well, at least the morning was.

'You were all over the house last night, Sam!' his mother informed him as he tried to eat his cereal in front of the television in the kitchen. 'You were pacing about in your sleep, opening and closing doors, and shouting, "It's not there! They've got it, Mel! They've got it! Where is it? Where's the helicopter?"'

Sam stopped mid-mouthful and looked up at his mother. 'I didn't, did I?' he asked, suddenly remembering the disc hidden in the curtain.

'You did!"

Sam put his cornflakes down and ran into the front

room, with his mother calling after him, 'Now you've spilled milk all over the table! What's on your mind? What on earth have you been up to?'

Sam dropped to the floor and rolled towards the curtain, feeling along the hem. The disc was still there. He breathed a sigh of relief and looked up to see his mother standing in the doorway.

'What are you doing now? Why are you rolling along the floor?'

'Nothing!'

'Nothing?'

'I've lost my homework. I thought Puffin might have hidden it behind the curtain,' said Sam, his skin shivering momentarily at the name of his cat.

'Oh, really?' said Mrs Piper suspiciously, lifting an eyebrow.

As soon as she spoke he realized he had given a pathetic excuse for his actions. 'Well, you know what Puffin's like. He chews things up, hides them, and then looks as innocent as anything!'

'Well, what are you doing rolling over the carpet in your pyjamas, like a three-year-old?'

Sam glanced at the top of the piano, and, noticing a hairy demon with two sly, half-closed eyes said, 'I thought Puffin was going to launch himself at my face.'

There was a deep-throated growl from the cat, as

he realized that his two humans were not only invading his space but also daring to stare at him.

'All right!' Mrs Piper declared, knowing that the feline from hell might shortly launch itself at her. 'I'm looking away and backing out through the door . . . you crazy animal!'

Sam, half crouching as he moved beneath the piano keys to keep out of sight, crawled back to the kitchen where his mother was waiting for him. Sam wasn't ready for her next outburst.

'I want you to stop these ridiculous missions, Sam. For goodness' sake, there are grown men and women out there who do daft things for MI21 without you and Mel getting involved.'

'What missions?'

'You know exactly what I'm talking about . . . MI21 and Uncle Jack. You scare me to death half the time. Haven't you got enough to keep you occupied with the Mel and Sam Spectacular Show, without risking your lives working for a secret service?'

Well, what could he say? Sam finished his cereal and then went to cut some bread. He really didn't want to be drawn into this conversation: he knew it would probably end in an argument and that wasn't what he wanted today. He just wanted to rest. When Sam picked up the bread knife his mother was temporarily diverted.

'Why don't you use the "plastic" bread? It's easier. You'll cut yourself on that knife!' she said as she watched him slice the bread on the board.

'I don't want the "plastic" bread. This tastes much better than that rubbish.'

'It's not rubbish. It's multiwhite.' She busied herself around the sink area. 'You're the only boy I know who buys his own loaf of bread for the weekend. Anyway, don't change the subject! I was talking about these missions you go on. They've got to stop, Sam. Your dad will be furious when he gets back.'

'I didn't change the subject, Mum. You did! You were the one who started talking about bread.'

'No more missions, Sam!'

'We didn't go on a mission, Mum. We were given something to hide and then things went wrong. But we think it'll be all right, now . . . for a while.'

'For a while?'

'Until we're able to give the thing to Uncle Jack.'

'What thing, Sam?'

'Can't say.'

'Well, where is it?'

'Can't say,' they both said together.

'Why can't you tell me? I'm your mother!'

'Because they might be listening.'

'Who might?'

'The people who are after it.'

'But how can they listen, Sam?'

'You know what Uncle Jack told you when he sent us to Apple's. They know where we live. That means they may have been in the house. When we were out.' Here Sam was economical with the truth.

'May have been in the house?'

'They *may* have been.'

'Good grief!' Mrs Piper left the sink and started pacing around the kitchen. 'There *were* little things out of place. Moved slightly. I thought it was you.' She raised her voice so that she could be heard in the front room. 'Or that ruddy cat of yours!' There was a distant sound of hissing and spitting.

'He's not my cat!'

'Well, he certainly isn't mine. And stop trying to change the subject!'

'But he's not!'

'How will they listen, these people who are after this 'thing'?'

Sam looked at his mother and let out a sigh. 'They may, but only may, have bugged the house.'

'Bugged? What do you mean? What with?'

'Microphones, of course!'

'Microphones?'

'And I suppose they could have installed cameras.'

'Cameras? Oh, my goodness! Where, where?' She looked frantically around the kitchen.

'Well, we don't know if they have planted anything at all.'

'But they could have! Where would they put these things?'

'Can't tell. They're so tiny these days. They could be anywhere. But I don't think they really had time to put in a surveillance system.'

'Stop it, Sam! We've got to go. *I've* got to go!' Sam watched his mother building up towards whirlwind mode. On Saturdays she often managed to relax, but now she was losing it again. Cereal boxes were stuffed into cupboards. Dishes were virtually thrown into the dishwasher. Her dressing gown was beginning to swirl as she moved rapidly round the room. Sam picked up the bread and clutched it to his chest in case it ended up in the fridge or the dishwasher, rather than the bread bin. Finally his mother dashed out of the room, shouting, 'I've got to get out of here!' But then she suddenly returned.

'Sam, where can I change? There might be cameras anywhere – even in my bedroom! This is awful! I know, I'll change in the bathroom.'

Sam couldn't resist it. 'They might be in there too, Mum!'

'What, in the bathroom? No! They wouldn't!'

'Well, they can put bugs anywhere.'

'But that's sick! This is your fault, hiding that

blooming thing. Why didn't you just throw it away?'

'What thing?'

'The thing they're after!'

Sam suddenly realized that he had better not continue the conversation. He stood up and walked towards the door. 'I think I'll go and get changed as well, Mum.'

'How long do you think these bugs will be here?'

'If there are any.'

'If there are any.'

The Agents' Handbook warning, Rule 354 drifted back into his mind again: 'You may never see the microphone they've planted. It could have been there for years, or it might not be there at all!'

Sam looked at his worried mother and said, 'When this is all over MI21 will move in and remove any bugs from the house.'

'Well, when will it be over, Sam? For goodness' sake give the thing to Uncle Jack so we can get back to normal.'

'I will, Mum, as soon as he sends someone to collect it.'

'What a way to start a day!' his mother moaned, as she collapsed into a chair with her head in her hands.

Sam thought of the start to the day he had had yesterday. Attacked by their crazy cat; squirted with gas; dangled upside down under a roaring helicopter, just seconds away from a horrible death. Somehow his mother's bad start just didn't match up. She had no idea what had happened to him during Friday, nor the real details of any other day of the week for that matter. He couldn't tell her. She'd blow her top, stop him from seeing Mel and threaten to inform the police of the antics of MI21 in the area. He would love to talk through the whole harrowing ordeal, but he couldn't. MI21 would do that for him in a debriefing session, after this was all over.

He looked at her from the doorway. 'When's Dad coming home?'

'Tuesday. I hope to goodness he's able to keep to it. Then he'll be off work until next Saturday.'

'It will be nice to have him home, Mum.'

'Yes, it will. I wish he was here now.'

Sam glanced at his mother. Suddenly she looked very tired. The whirlwind had finally died out and now there wasn't even a breeze. She slumped into a kitchen chair.

'Mum, I've got to go and see Mel,' sighed Sam.

'What, now?'

'Yeah. We've got a performance next weekend, remember? Down at Rundale Hall. For the old people.'

'Oh, yes. I'd forgotten.'

'We've got to work on the programme.'

He turned and walked up the stairs. Until that moment he had forgotten all about next week's Mel and Sam Spectacular Show. There was a lot to do, even without a team of Mad Skunks chasing them!

Sam wanted to have the most fabulous show ever seen anywhere in the country; and it would all develop from the Mel and Sam Spectacular Show and the amazing illusions he and Mel invented. But in his daydreams he also saw another future: one in MI21. Mel's family connections with Uncle Jack had meant Sam had been drawn in to an amazing double life on the very edge of a secret government organization. Sam felt both excited and confused. What would he do in the future? Create a world-famous show or be a secret agent?

Or both?

The telephone rang downstairs. He heard his mother talking before she shouted up to him.

'Sam, Mel's going out with her mother, shopping, so you don't need to go to hers now. Says she'll come round here at 2.00. That OK?'

Sam was trying to pull a sock on to his left foot. 'Yes, Mum!' He heard her carry on talking, finishing with 'Fine, pet. See you later. Bye!'

After Sam's mum had put the phone down, she turned and called up the stairs, 'You can come shopping with me if you like, Sam.'

'No way, thanks!'

'Pardon?'

'I said, 'Not today, thanks!''

'But Mel's gone shopping.'

'Mel likes shopping!'

'You like shopping sometimes.'

'Only when I want something.'

'Don't you want anything?' his mother asked hopefully.

'I only want to think about this show we've got next weekend!'

'Oh, of course. I know you like to practise. I'll be your audience during the week, if you'd like me to.'

'Yes, Mum, that would be great. Tuesday night OK?'

'Should be fine. Right, I'm going to change now, Sam. In the cupboard under the stairs. There won't be any cameras or bugs under there, will there?'

'No, Mum.' *No bugs there, Mum, just great big, black, hairy spiders!*

Mel spent most of her time that morning at the White-water Shopping Centre. Like so many others, once you had stepped though the plate-glass doors you could be in any town, anywhere in the country, but Mel's mum liked shopping, so they had always spent a considerable amount of time there choosing their favourite clothes or must-have bargains. Then, right at the last minute, Mel's mum would declare that she wasn't sure, or that she and Mel didn't really need any more clothes – there wasn't much money to spend. Sometimes Mel found it boring, but it was good to be out with her mum, so she tried not to complain; not too often, anyway.

Shopping made them hungry, so Mel and her mother made their way to The Cascade: a vast eating area near the middle of the shopping centre, with what seemed like hundreds of chairs and tables. They chose a table near the Italian counter. It was getting noisy.

Mel's mum gave her some money and shouted, 'You join the queue and I'll keep the table.'

Mel made her way through the throng, towards the food counter. As she was reading the crowded menu board more people brushed past. Then there was a push on her leg and as, she glanced down, Mel saw a briefcase lid suddenly spring open. Papers, pamphlets and pens fell around her feet.

A woman in dark glasses spoke. 'Oh, no! See what you've done!'

Mel looked up at her, thinking that somehow she was at fault. 'I'm sorry,' she said, kneeling down to pick up the woman's belongings, 'I just didn't see you. I was looking up at the . . . ' Mel froze. As the woman knelt down to help, Mel could see that she was wearing a dark wig, heavy make-up and thick red lipstick. There was a slight scar to the side of her mouth. An attempt had been made to cover it up, but at this distance Mel could see it very clearly. The woman looked as though she was in disguise.

Mel could feel her heart beating hard inside her chest, but the woman's voice was now quite soft and reassuring. 'Don't stop what you are doing and don't look round or run away. You are being watched. There are two of them in here now. They have been following you all morning. We have been watching them and you. We are here to help if necessary, but we would rather stay out of the way.'

Mel wanted to look around but she knew that in doing so she might give the game away. She tested the woman with a question. 'Who is watching me?'

'Mad Skunks.'

'Why?'

'Disc.'

Mel kept her eyes on the floor. 'Why hasn't some-body collected it yet?' she asked.

'Because the Skunks are supposed to have it.'

'What!'

'You've got to let them have it, Mel. They have to have the disc.'

'What?'

'Give it to them!' she hissed. The woman put the

last pen in the briefcase, snapped it shut and stood up. 'Thank you,' she said pleasantly. Then she smiled, smoothed down her skirt and walked briskly in the direction of the exit.

Melanie stood there with her mouth open. All manner of thoughts raced through her head. Now she had got to get to Sam . . . fast!

CHAPTER 8

Mum nails the disc!

WHEN MRS PIPER ANSWERED THE DOOR early that afternoon, Mel burst in with a 'Hello, Mrs Piper. Where's Sam?' and sped towards the kitchen.

'He's upstairs, love . . . '

Melanie shot up the stairs towards Sam's bedroom. Mrs Piper's voice trailed on in the background. 'I hope the pair of you aren't in trouble again. I've told him he's not to go on any more missions!'

Mel wasn't listening. She flung open the door to Sam's room and launched herself inside. Sam jumped with alarm and dropped part of a model of an illusionist's box. It fell to the floor and the lid snapped off.

'Aaw, Mel!'

'Sam, listen. You are not going to believe what happened today!'

She sat on the edge of the bed and began to tell him about her trip to the shopping centre. When Mel recounted what the woman with the briefcase had said, Sam started to walk around the room, thinking out loud.

'She said to hand the disc over?'

'Yes. And she even knew my name!'

'But this doesn't make sense. Why should we give it to them?' asked Sam.

'I don't know, Sam.'

'Did she say she was from MI21?'

'No, but she said that they had been watching two Skunks following me around all day.'

'So she must have been one of our lot then. Have you ever seen her before?'

Mel shook her head. 'No, but then she was pretty heavily disguised, and MI21 wouldn't really send anybody who might be recognized, would they? She did have a scar on the side of her mouth, though.'

'But I don't understand why she is telling us to hand over the disc. Especially after all we went through yesterday!'

They both stayed silent for a while, until Mel said, 'There must be something on the disc that MI21 want the Skunks to find out.'

'That doesn't make sense,' Sam blurted out. 'Why would that agent, Vardoo, be chasing two of them to get the disc if they were supposed to have it anyway?

'Perhaps Uncle Jack just thinks we're in too much danger and feels it's better if we just hand it over. Maybe it's not so important after all. That's the other thing, Mel. Why didn't anyone from MI21 come to get the disc off us? They always say they'll be here soon, but they've never arrived.'

'Uncle Jack always has a reason, Sam.'

'A great organization like MI21 could rescue the man on the moon if they had to. Surely they could take a disc off two kids!'

'But wait a minute, Sam. What if the woman in the shopping centre was a Skunk?'

'What?'

'Think about it. She may actually be a Skunk who's trying to trick us into giving away the disc!'

'But, she knew your name. This is all so confusing!'

'Well, it could have been Claudette. Pretending to be an MI21 agent when all the time she's a Skunk. *She* knows my name, and yours. Anyway, the Skunks know who we are, where we live and probably the names of all our relatives and friends, too!'

At that moment the door flew open and Sam's mum walked in.

'So it's a disc, is it?' his mother demanded.

Sam was outraged. 'Mum, you've been listening!

What are you doing listening at the door?'

'I didn't have to "listen", Sam. You were both talking so loudly I couldn't help but hear every word. I shouldn't think these "Skunks" need any bugs around this house; they could have heard you out in the street!'

Mel turned to Sam as if he had betrayed some secret. 'Bugs? What have you been saying, Sam?'

'Only telling me there might be bugs in the house,' Mrs Piper informed her. 'Microphones or even cameras. Here in my house!'

Mel stared at Sam, aghast, but before she could say anything, he explained, 'Look, I didn't just "tell" Mum. She was asking questions about what they were after and I said we couldn't talk about it because they might be listening. Mum knows they may have been in the house.'

'I do now. I won't be able to sleep a wink all night. And I'll have to change under the bedclothes!'

Mel shot Sam a questioning look.

'Mum thinks there may be cameras around the house watching our every move.'

'But why would they have put cameras up, Sam?' Mel asked.

Sam's mother answered straight away. 'Oh, that's so they could see where you've hidden the thing that they wanted!'

Mel looked at Sam again. His hands gestured his innocence.

Mrs Piper continued. 'But now I know what the 'thing' is, don't I? It's a disc, and Mel says that MI21 want you to hand it over to these Skunks.'

Sam put a finger to his lips. 'Shh, Mum, you don't know who's listening!'

Mrs Piper took a deep breath. 'I want the disc, Sam! I want you to give me the disc and I'll give it to these Skunk people, then they'll leave us alone.'

'But, Mum, you don't understand.'

'But, Mum, nothing. I want that disc. I'll pass it on and then you can forget all this and start practising for your show at the weekend.'

'And exactly how are you going to "pass it on", Mum? Have you got an address you can send it to – Skunk House, Skunk Lane, Skunkton?'

'Sam, that's enough!'

Then, to Mel's surprise, Sam moved towards the door saying, 'You're right, Mum. I've had enough of this. Let's get rid of it, then we can get on with our show. I don't want the disc any more!'

Mel jumped up in a panic. 'Sam, what are you doing? We can't just throw it away!'

'No, Mel. Mum's right. Everything will be OK if the disc is gone.'

Mel couldn't believe what she was hearing, but

then she noticed Sam's right hand on his chest. He was rattling his thumb and middle finger against his sweater, out of his mum's sight.

In any magic or illusionist's show it is vital that secret signs are passed between the magician and his assistant. Mel and Sam had worked out quite a few, and this was one of them. *Everything is OK. Go along with it. I know what I'm doing.* Mel continued to protest, but her eyes now held a twinkle and she wondered what Sam had up his sleeve.

Sam's mother went to follow him as he left the room but, when Mel saw the expression on Sam's face, Mel distracted her by bursting into floods of tears and apologizing to Mrs Piper for getting her involved. Within two minutes Sam was back in the room holding a computer disc.

'Are you sure that's it?' asked his mother. 'How do you know it's the right one?'

'It's got two green dots on it. Must be some sort of code they use,' Sam replied as he handed the disc to his mother.

Mel smiled to herself as she recognized it. *Yes,* she thought, *it's a special code all right. It means that Sam has just given his mother his homework disc!*

Mrs Piper turned it over in her hand and asked what was on it. Sam told her there was important information stored on it that they couldn't open on their computers.

His mother suddenly stood up and marched out of the room. 'Right, time to get rid of this thing and then we can get back to normal.'

'What are you going to do with it, Mrs Piper?' Melanie asked.

'Oh, you'll soon see!'

There was nothing remotely complicated about handing over a top-secret disc to a group of underworld crooks, according to Sam's mum. They didn't have to return it secretively to Skunk Headquarters, wherever that may have been. Or scale fences. Or drug snarling Rottweilers with laced pieces of meat. Or even dangle from a length of rope from the thirteenth floor to break into offices in the dead of night. No. Mrs Piper's solution to the problem was quite simple. She went under the stairs, opened the toolbox and took out a hammer and two nails. She then marched out of the front door to the garden gate. There, so it could be clearly seen, she nailed the disc to the gatepost, not through the hole in the middle, but by smashing a nail right through the disc itself. Mel and Sam watched in amazement as she then went inside, returning with a cardboard sign, which she hammered to the post above it.

The sign clearly read, in luminous felt pen, *'SKUNKS! Here it is. This is the disc you want.'*

The children then followed Mrs Piper back into the kitchen.

'Mum, the disc won't work again now. You've hammered a nail right through it!'

'Sam, do you really think I care? I can't read what's on the disc. You can't read what's on the disc and, more importantly, *they* can't read what's on the disc! So I've really done a great job in helping MI21 out, haven't I? Perhaps they'll give me an award for it!' With this Mrs Piper turned and busied herself in a cupboard full of tins and packets.

Sam indicated to Mel that they should leave. Back up in his room the children breathed a sigh of relief.

'So, is the real disc still hidden, Sam?'

'Yes, safely stashed away until we decide what to do with it. Unlike my homework – I'll have to do all that again!'

'Oh, well, I'll help you with it later, but we can't do anything about it now. Let's concentrate on the show. Tell me about this box you're working on.'

Sam showed Mel his model of a magic box and tried to explain what it would do if only he could get help to build the real thing. He wanted it to be on castor wheels and made so the four sides of the box – hinged along the base – would fold down to conceal a secret, human-sized compartment.

'Sam, this is brilliant! But, who's going to go in the base?'

'You, or me. We could take it in turns.'

'It's going to be very squashed. Will we be able to breathe in there?'

'Yes, there'll be plenty of holes drilled in the top of the compartment so we can breathe and see what's going on.'

'This is just what we need to develop the show. How long do you think it will take to build?'

'Could be ages yet. Weeks perhaps.'

'Oh. That means we can't use it in the next few shows we've got coming up.'

'Well, the box is really simple, even though it's got a false bottom. It's really only a hollow base, four sides and a lid. If we had help and a few days off we might be able to get it finished.'

'Your dad built the last piece of equipment for us. Do you think he'd help with this one?'

'I dunno. He had more time before. Now he spends weeks away at meetings and conferences.' Sam could see the disappointment in Mel's eyes. 'He's supposed to be coming home on Tuesday, though. We'll give him a day's rest and then ask him. He might do it if he's got nothing else to do. Though I expect Mum's got a long list of jobs for him to tackle – he'll probably take one look at that and then disappear again for a fortnight!'

In the distance the phone rang as Mel suggested they ought to make some attempt to practise for next weekend's show.

'And we'd better check our email. What with all this chasing around we haven't done that for over a week!'

'Yes, we were going to revamp our Spectacular Show website as well. We've forgotten about it completely!'

'Oh, I don't want to do that yet. It takes ages. There's never enough time.'

'I'd rather be working on practical things, like this box.'

Sam's mother suddenly called up from downstairs. 'Mel, your mother's been on the phone. She says you and Sam have got to be at your house by 4.00 as Uncle Jack wants a word with both of you. You tell him I've nailed the disc to the gatepost and that Sam's not to go on any more missions. Do you hear me?'

'Yes, Mrs Piper!'

'Yes, Mum!'

Mel grinned at Sam and whispered, 'No more missions, eh? Pigs might fly! And Miss Pinkley might wear sunglasses, and go clubbing in a black dress and high-heeled boots!'

And they both burst into fits of giggles.

CHAPTER 9

Uncle Jack and the unexpected truth!

AT MEL'S HOUSE THAT AFTERNOON, THE children heard a car draw up outside, followed quickly by two vans. Mel and Sam ran to the window to watch as the doors opened and several 'window cleaners' stepped out on to the pavement. They started to untie ladders, unload buckets and rinse out cloths. Of course, had anyone been looking closely, they might have noticed that the 'window cleaners' were wearing cleverly disguised wires and earpieces, and were frequently checking the street for suspicious persons. But, naturally, had anyone got that close they would have been knocked out by a squirt of special-formula window-cleaner spray before they knew what had hit them. Next, a large man with a cigar in one hand, and a bucket in the other, walked down the path towards Mel's front door.

'Mum, it's Uncle Jack. He's come here! He's actually come here!'

'Oh, for goodness' sake! I thought he'd just phone.' Mrs Eastwood dashed to the window to peer through the net curtain. 'Oh, good grief! Look at them all. Wandering about all over the place. What on earth was he thinking? What will the neighbours say?'

'But he is your brother, Mum!' scolded Melanie.

'Yes, but look at him, swaggering down the drive with a bucket on his arm. Does he really think he looks like a window cleaner? How's he going to do that job with a cigar in his hand?'

With this the doorbell rang, and when Mel ran to open it there stood her favourite uncle. She was fascinated by him, mainly because of the mysterious life he led, and this enthusiasm had also infected Sam. The two of them stood there smiling, speechless.

'Any chance of a bucket of warm water?' Jack's voice boomed above the silent children.

'Oh, yes,' shouted Mrs Eastwood from a distance. 'All over your head!'

'Nice to see you as well, sis!' laughed Uncle Jack with a mischievous grin. He ran his fingers through his thick hair and entered the house.

While Uncle Jack was filling his bucket from the sink, two of his colleagues entered carrying a large box complete with a substantial number of dangling wires.

Uncle Jack's sister raised her eyebrows.

'Ah! Jeanette, these are two of my crew . . . er . . . Peter and Simon.' Uncle Jack reached into his pocket and pulled out a folded sheet of paper. He held it up for the others to see. It said: *They will trawl the house checking for listening devices or cameras. We are to talk only about the weather and the coming summer holidays until we get the all-clear.* Uncle Jack then nodded to his two colleagues and they immediately went to the base of the stairs to start their search.

As the other agents left the room, Jack Sanders settled himself in a chair and began to tell a wonderful story, to fool anyone who might be listening, about rescuing his koi carp from a determinedly hungry heron.

After a few minutes they heard rapid high-pitched notes coming from the hall: two high notes followed by a lower one, repeated until the signal was switched off.

'Seems they've found something,' whispered Uncle Jack.

Sam stood up, intrigued by what was going on. 'Can we go and see?'

'Of course you can. But quietly!' Jack waved an arm towards the door, encouraging them to go and watch. Sam and Mel moved across the room and stood at the door. One of the men was moving a small piece of equipment through the air. It was about the size of a mobile phone but was attached, by cables, to a large

box on the floor. The other man was on his knees looking underneath the hall table. He took out a screw-
driver from his trouser pocket and levered something
away from the underside of the table. He held it up. It
was a small black button with a short metallic arm
attached to it. His colleague took out a small metal
container from the box on the floor, dropped the item
inside and closed the lid firmly.

'Well done, you two,' whispered Uncle Jack, who
was now standing behind Mel and Sam. 'What sort of
bug was it?'

'Oh, nothing exciting, just a standard CRX 23. It was
stuck to the hall table, right underneath the telephone.'

Mel looked at her uncle. 'So they could hear incom-
ing and outgoing messages?'

'Maybe, Mel, but the CRX 23 is really only any good
at listening to voices in a room.'

'Can they hear us now?'

'Not when the bug's in that box. But keep your
voices down in case any of the other rooms are
bugged.'

Suddenly the agent with the cabled device gave a
signal not to talk and tilted his equipment in Uncle
Jack's direction so that he could see the flickering
needle and flashing diode. Silently Uncle Jack pointed
to the telephone, and on receiving a nod from the

technician he indicated that the phone should be removed. It was then disconnected and taken to one of the cars outside.

'Wow!' said Sam quietly. 'So the phone was bugged, after all.'

When Sam, Mel and her mother were sitting down again in the lounge Uncle Jack explained how sometimes a device may be used as a decoy, so that anyone finding it will think that once it's removed the area is safe. Yet, as in this case, there was another device inside the telephone, and this one would have been able to monitor all calls in and out.

Soon Simon and Peter returned to check the remaining rooms, while everyone sat in silence, watching and waiting for the alarm to go off.

Finally one of them said, 'Right, that's it, boss. All clear.' And the two of them started to pack away the equipment.

'Will you check our house too?' asked Sam. 'Only my mum's really worried about being spied on.'

'We will, Sam, but not tonight. We've done this house first because it's vital that I talk to you and I needed to make sure that nobody else was listening.'

'So that's why you didn't phone,' said Mrs Eastwood.

'And we thought you just wanted to see us,' said Mel.

'I know, I know. I agree I haven't been to see you much recently, but . . . you know . . . '

'Yes, Jack, you're "too busy". Everybody's too busy these days to spend any time with friends and relatives,' Mrs Eastwood replied sarcastically.

Just then there came the sound of another car drawing up and stopping. Doors opened and voices drifted through the window. One of them was a woman's. 'Will you get your hands off me. Ruddy cheek!' The voice sounded familiar.

'Just helping you out, ma'am!' came the reply.

'I didn't want to be helped in!'

'Ah,' said Uncle Jack. 'We have another visitor!' He stood and walked towards the front door.

Mel and Sam shot to the window in time to see Sam's mum being escorted to Mel's front door by two burly 'gas engineers'.

As soon as she saw Uncle Jack standing before her, the shouting began. 'What are you doing with my Sam? No more missions! I told him to tell you. It's no good you getting your monkeys round to kidnap me. He's not going on any more missions!'

When Mrs Piper scuttled into the lounge and saw Mel and Sam with Mrs Eastwood she calmed down a little. 'There you are, Sam. I thought for a moment when they kidnapped me that something awful had happened to you.'

'You haven't been kidnapped, Mrs Piper,' Uncle Jack offered.

'Oh, no? When I answered the door they told me to come with them. These men from the "gas company" held out a card which just had the words "Sam, Mel and Uncle Jack" written on it. They wouldn't explain anything. I barely had time to get a coat on before they bundled me into a dark-windowed van. I have never been so frightened in my life!'

'Sit down, Mrs Piper. I think you need to listen to what I have to say. That's why I've had you brought here.'

'Ah, so I *have* been "brought here" for a reason.'

'Yes.'

'Well, if you want Sam to go on a dangerous mission, the answer's no!'

When Mrs Piper had settled herself into the last armchair, Uncle Jack told the mums about the rescuing of the disc; the chase through the streets; Skunks tracking the children down and planting a tracking device; the search through the two homes; the chase to school; hiding in Apple's safe house and then, of course, Friday. 'I'm afraid I have to inform you, that yesterday both children were actually captured by the Mad Skunks and carted off from Whitewater.'

The two mothers looked at each other, mouths open.

Uncle Jack continued. 'Of course you will under-stand that we cannot disclose all details, but it is suffi-cient for me to say that they were both captured and were in mortal danger.'

'Mortal danger! You didn't tell me this, Sam,' said his mum.

'Nor you, Melanie!' said Mrs Eastwood.

'We didn't want you to be worried,' Sam explained.

'Didn't want us to be worried? We've had an awful week, with the two of you in all sorts of trouble!'

'You wouldn't want to know about yesterday. We escaped and we're here now, so that's all that matters.'

'No more missions! I'm telling you straight: no more missions!'

'How did you escape then, if you were captured?' asked Melanie's mum.

Now, the Agents' Handbook, Rule 321 section 3b is very clear on giving out information:

'There are times when it is best to give only basic information, even to friends and relatives. They may otherwise become confused, worried or may want to change the course of action.

There are also times when it is best not to elaborate. In fact it is often better not to disclose all the facts. Keep some of the truth to yourself.'

Sam looked at Uncle Jack and saw a faint, hardly

perceptible nod. 'Well, I think we were sprayed with something to knock us out as we walked to school. When I woke up I was completely tied up with ropes!'

'I was on a seat, with my legs tied to it,' Melanie chimed in, realizing what she had to say, and how carefully she had to do it so as not to alarm their parents. 'But fancy tying Sam up with ropes, of all things. He thought he was practising for the show!' She tried a laugh, but nobody else smiled, except Sam.

'Anyway,' Sam continued, 'when this fellow, Mad Skunk Skuda, wasn't looking, I loosened the ropes, undid the knots and escaped. And Mel threw a can of Coke at him and knocked him out of the er ... *vehicle.*'

'What?' asked Mrs Eastwood, looking at Mel. 'What vehicle?'

Melanie cringed. 'Well, it was pretty big . . . and it was travelling fast near a wood . . . and when he stood in the doorway I threw a couple of cans and knocked him out of it . . . '

'Mel used a voice impersonation and shouted to the driver to stop. She did and we jumped out and ran like heck!'

'She?' asked Mrs Piper.

'Yes, Mum. The driver was a woman.'

'When we jumped out I shouted in Mad Skunk Skuda's voice that the police were coming and she shot off. We ran to Littleton post office without stopping and called for a lift!' Seeing that their explanation had been believed, Mel sighed inwardly with relief and smiled at Sam.

Uncle Jack nodded his head and was also about to smile, when suddenly his sister turned to him and said, 'And all of this is about a blooming computer disc that's in Mel and Sam's keeping? Well, why haven't you been to collect the wretched thing, Jack?'

But as Jack opened his mouth to speak, Mrs Piper burst out, 'Well, you'll be glad to hear, Jeanette, that I was so fed up with this saga that I got the disc off Sam and nailed it to our front gatepost!'

Uncle Jack shot forward in his seat with a roar. 'You've done what?'

He shot a glance at Sam and just caught him signalling secretly with his thumb and middle finger on his chest: *Everything is OK. Go along with it. I know what I'm doing.*

Uncle Jack kept a straight face and continued, 'Mrs Piper, do you realize what you have done?'

'Yes, I do. I've nailed it to the post with a sign saying, *"SKUNKS! Here it is. This is the disc you want."* I'm fed up with the danger Sam's in, and Melanie for that matter! We don't want the disc. They do. Now no one can use the disc because I've driven a nail right through it so it will never work again.'

Uncle Jack sat back, putting his hands together

over his large stomach. 'So the disc is ruined?'

Mrs Piper nodded. 'And it will be even more ruined when they try to take the nail out with a claw hammer.'

'It's time for me to explain something to all of you, particularly Mel and Sam.' Uncle Jack stood up and walked to the window, lighting his cigar, which let out a great cloud of smoke that wafted around his head.

'Oh, for goodness' sake, Jack, don't smoke that thing in here. You'll set the smoke alarm off!'

Uncle Jack appeared not to hear. 'We have an agent working deep within the Skunk Empire. She passed on information to the Skunks that a valuable consignment would be arriving in Hull soon. The informer indicated that the contents would be of special interest to the Mad Skunk Empire and that at least one Skunk unit should be put on the case. She also added that MI21 were not sending details electronically as they suspected a double agent was working in the communications department. All details would be on a disc. Our agent told the Skunks who would be delivering it what day it would travel and the registration number of the car being used. Hence the chase and crash on the edge of Whitewater.'

'But, I don't understand,' said Mel. 'Why would your agent tell the Mad Skunks about a delivery to Hull?'

'Because it's a trap. We want them to know when the consignment will arrive. When they try to hijack it we will step in and arrest a whole unit of Skunks and hopefully get a ton of information out of them.'

'So the Mad Skunks have got to have the disc?' Mel had now gone white.

'Yes, Mel, otherwise the plot will fail.'

'Wait a minute!' Sam's voice was now raised. 'You mean that the Skunks were to get the disc all along? That we weren't supposed to hold on to it for the week?'

Everyone looked at Uncle Jack. He walked forward again and swirls of smoke billowed around his head.

'You were better than we could ever have imagined. We thought you would give them a good run for their money but assumed that they would find the disc during the first night, yet, unbelievably, you lost them and that made them even more determined.'

'But we were in danger, Uncle Jack. Why didn't you help us?' asked Melanie.

'Yes, Jack,' agreed her mother, 'these two could have been injured or worse!'

Sam wasn't listening. *All of that was for nothing,* he thought. *We nearly got killed . . . for nothing! MI21 expected us to fail!*

'You expected us to fail!' Sam shouted angrily. He got to his feet, 'Mel, we weren't expected to succeed!

Give this mission to Mel and Sam because they will fail! They're the best ones we've got for failing!' Tears were sparkling in his eyes now. Mel leaned forward, putting her face in her hands. 'If you want something done wrong, give it to Mel and Sam! They'll lose the disc for you. They might get chased, tormented and squirted with gas for a week, but they'll lose the disc for you. They might even get captured and tied up for a bit of fun. They might get dangled on a rope, but they'll give the disc away ... eventually. You never know, they might even die for it!' The tears of frustration flowed over Sam's cheeks. He wiped them away with both palms. All his dreams of the future had now gone. He no longer wanted any part in the MI21 organization. Now he hated them. All of them.

Melanie jumped up in front of her uncle, her eyes watery and red. 'You could have sent an agent in to pick it up at any time, Uncle Jack. The Skunks would then have left us alone and gone chasing your man instead. But, no, it was more important that the Skunks got this rotten disc! Trudy Blueshoes at the Ministry of Information knew we were in trouble, she said we were about to *ride a tiger* ! I didn't understand what she meant until I thought about it later. If you ride a tiger you have to stay on it because you'll be in even bigger trouble if you get off! And that's what you did to us!' All colour had drained from her face and she felt herself start to shake.

Uncle Jack stood up and made to put his arm around her but she fled across the room to Sam. They stood facing him.

'I can understand why you are upset,' Jack said patiently, 'but you are still "riding the tiger"! You can't get off yet. We have not finished.'

'Oh, yes, I think they jolly well have, Jack!' his sister informed him.

'Jeanette, please let me finish what I have to say, especially now that the disc has been nailed to a gatepost. I'm afraid that the Skunks won't be too pleased about that.'

'That disc . . . ' began Sam, but Jack silenced him with a wave of his hand.

'I know, Sam! Please let me finish. As I was saying: you were initially asked to help in the chase. This was so we could see the speed at which you could get across town, and also to give you a little taste of action, because soon you will become more involved in the organization. That was the sole purpose. We did not expect you to come away with the disc.'

'But we did.'

'Yes, Mel, and you cannot imagine the pride I felt when I heard about that. We then held hasty meetings deciding what to do. We could easily have come in to get the disc, but the Skunks would have been watching. They would have been very suspicious and would have left the project alone. We decided we wanted to use the situation to our best advantage.'

'To your advantage! What about them?' asked Jack's sister. 'It's our homes that have been under threat.'

'Yes, but we have had agents close by for some time, just in case anything went wrong. They have been watching from a distance. And now, by watching and filming we have even more information on these Mad Skunks and how they operate. And we still have a chance of capturing a whole unit at Hull. The way I see it, it's short-term danger for long-term gain.'

'I still don't understand,' said Mel. 'Have we failed or not?'

'Not at all, Mel. You may have delayed the false information reaching the Skunks, but you have greatly increased your own ratings within the MI21 organization.' Everyone watched Jack Sanders step forward again, streams of blue smoke swirling around him. 'As we watched you we became aware of your extraordinary skills. You were actually succeeding where a great team in MI21 had expected you to fail. Now, here was our dilemma: do we help you two to fail, or do we see how far you can go in succeeding? In our control office we had people getting cross because you'd been too clever and the Skunks hadn't managed to get the disc off you, and others shouting their support because you were doing a wonderful job. They were actually starting to predict how long you would hold out. That's when we realized we would have to be prepared to act quickly if anything went wrong. But then, at the end, you made a mistake. You didn't remember Rule 511: *"Never, never, ever follow the same route as the one you took the time before".'*

'It was my fault,' said Sam. ' I was tired from the previous day.'

'It wasn't your fault, Sam. You had both done a brilliant job and even then you managed to escape. Brilliant, just brilliant!'

'So where were your lot, Jack, when these children were doing a brilliant job of making their escape, hey?' asked his sister.

'Well, not too far away, actually. Only eighty miles.'

'Eighty miles! What help would that have been?'

'Well, we were equipped with a Harrier Jump Jet, Jeanette,' retorted Jack.

Sam and Mel remembered the end to the previous day's adventure – watching an impressive Harrier GR7 bank around the fields and hover near them.

Sam looked at Mel and then back at Uncle Jack. 'So, we did do a good job then?'

'You did an excellent job. Far better than expected! Proved many of our old fogies wrong. You're now well on the way into the "Next Stage" of your agent's training: the pair of you!'

'I'm telling you, Jack Sanders, my Sam is not to go on any more missions with your lot! This was the last time. So you can jolly well forget the "Next Stage".'

Jack turned to face her, with a smile on his face. 'Mrs Piper! What are we to do? You have ruined a multi million-pound exercise, designed to capture some of Europe's worst criminals in the trafficking of illegal goods, by destroying the information that would have led to their capture! How is this going to look in court, Mrs Piper?'

'Court? What are you talking about?'

'You have destroyed an MI21 exercise that would probably have saved the country a billion pounds. Small firms may now go out of business, jobs will be lost, and the criminals will become even more powerful. I imagine your photograph will be on the front of every newspaper. You'll be seen as a traitor to your country!'

'Traitor? Court? Newspapers? What are you talking about? I only wanted to protect my Sam!'

'I think Sam is well able to protect himself, Mrs Piper. You, however, have destroyed the key to this mission.'

Sam was now actually feeling sorry for his mother; she was looking so alarmed. He looked at Mel. Then, suddenly, he had the answer.

'Uncle Jack, I think I know what to do. We . . . well . . . we made a copy of the disc. There's another at home. We can give them that.'

Jack had, of course, seen Sam's secret sign and knew that the disc on the gate wasn't the real one. Now he was happy to play along with Sam's plan to help get his mother off the hook. Uncle Jack knew that although Sam was offering a copy, it was really the original disc.

Good plan, Sam!

Sam's mother looked very relieved that her talented son had been smart enough to copy the wretched disc.

Uncle Jack smiled, nodded his head and said, 'I think we have the answer, folks.' He turned and sat on the arm of one of the chairs before continuing. 'The Skunks must intercept a message that lets them know the hiding place of this disc.'

'How do we do that?' asked Sam.

'I know,' said Mel. 'MI21 haven't swept your house for bugs yet, so you could phone Uncle Jack from there and tell him where we've hidden the disc.'

'Good idea, Mel,' said Jack. 'I suggest Sam and Mrs Piper make sure they're both out of the house at some time during the day tomorrow, to give the Skunks easy access.'

'What about the disc my mum nailed to the gate?'

Sam asked, glancing at his mother.

'That must be removed immediately. If the Skunks see that we could really be in trouble. All our planning will have been for nothing!' exclaimed Uncle Jack, looking straight at Mrs Piper.

'Well, I'm sorry!' she replied. 'I just thought I was doing the best for everyone.' But Jack cut her short with a wave of his hand.

'We have much to do.'

He buttoned up his long black coat and kissed his sister on the cheek.

'Now, I'm sending some agents up to Sam's house to check that the phone there is bugged. I expect it is. It will not be removed. Sam, when you get home, let's say in 45 minutes, you are to phone my mobile. Explain that you and Mel are frightened and that you want the disc collected. Say exactly where it is: that way the Mad Skunks can find it easily, and cause the least amount of damage.'

Uncle Jack made towards the door, but turned back to the children. 'Now, tomorrow I want you to relax. Forget the disc and practise for your show at the weekend.

'You know about our show?' Melanie asked.

'Of course. I know a lot about you two. I watch and listen more than you imagine!'

'What do you mean?'

Jack Sanders smiled at his niece. 'Keep your website up to date. You need to do a little more to it. Change the diary at the very least. Remember: *'Never neglect your skills. Whatever you can do well, develop it and make it better. And when you have made it better – make it better still, until you are the best and then never let go! Hold your head up proudly and say, 'I can do this. This is my area. You may have your skills but these are mine. I aim to be The Number One. And when I am there I will never let go, and even then – I will make it better still!'* Agents' Handbook, Rule 241 section 2d!

'Ah. I almost forgot! Perhaps you two would like to follow me.' He led them down the drive towards one of the 'window cleaner's' vans. He asked them to climb in the back, while he got into a front seat. There, between them, stood two plants, in pots.

'Three weeks ago I was in Africa . . . '

'Africa! I thought you were the European Operations Director?' interrupted Mel.

'Yes, but Mel, you must remember that our operations don't stop at the European borders. When we have goods coming in or going out we have to follow them.

'Anyway, we came across this village where the last tree had just been cut down to punish the villagers. It lay shattered on the ground. People were still crying, as it had been so special to them. The oldest man in the village, Mamello, told me the dreadful story of how all the rainforest in that area was destroyed, until all that remained was this sacred tree. I will tell you the tale, one day, when we have time.

'However, Mamello gave me two cuttings from the tree. He hoped I would look after them, and when they are as tall as a man he wants me to return to help start the replanting of the forest.'

Jack looked fondly at the children as they both reached forward to touch the tender leaves.

'Was it Mad Skunks who cut down the forest?'

'We don't think so, Sam, but they were criminals who have been supplying the Skunk Empire with all manner of things. The beauties of the earth mean nothing to some, compared with the chance to make money.

'I promised Mamello I would give the cuttings to two people who would relish the responsibility of helping to replant a rainforest.'

He looked the two children in the eyes. 'You are to look after these. Water and feed them, and when they are big enough, in a few years' time, perhaps all three of us will take them back and plant them where they came from.'

'What, to Africa?'

'Maybe, Mel.'

'Wowie!'

Then, before they knew it, Uncle Jack had kissed Mel on the cheek, and shaken Sam's hand, and the children were left standing on the pavement with the plant pots nestling in their arms, as a small fleet of window-cleaning and gas-company vans moved quietly down the street. Mel and Sam stared after them until the last one disappeared around the corner.

But they hadn't finished yet. In what seemed a very short while Sam was at home phoning Uncle Jack, as arranged. While far beyond Whitewater a Mad Skunk smiled, thumping the air in celebration: the disc was found. It was tucked away in the hem of a long curtain, and soon it would be theirs!

CHAPTER 10

Swap

AT JUST AFTER 9.00 P.M., SAM WAS IN HIS bedroom practising for the show in his magician's coat. He carefully placed small items into the many secret pockets in the flowing garment. Some of the inside pockets were quite large, but he particularly liked to use the small ones on the sleeves, and though his hands were quick he had to practise many times so he knew exactly where the entrance to each pocket lay.

It was not just the speed of his movements that Sam used to deceive the observer's eye; he often distracted his audience with his other hand or a funny remark. In a moment his free hand would dip into the pocket and conceal or retrieve an object, to gasps of astonishment.

Sam watched himself in the full-length mirror as

he made a long modelling balloon appear. He was perfecting his trick of bursting a balloon to reveal a ball of crunched-up silk handkerchiefs.

He looked around for another balloon to work with. Instantly his eyes were drawn to a small pile of computer discs on top of his desk. He lost concentration and began to think about the one hidden away in the hem of the curtain.

Why didn't we see anything interesting on the disc when we looked last time? We need to have another try. But we're supposed to let the disc go.

He started to pace the room. An idea had come to him. He had a vague memory of a strange silver square and a number on the surface of the original disc. But did he have time to do anything about it? *We have to swap the discs. The Mad Skunks won't know a copy from the original. There might be something else. Perhaps we should keep the one in the curtain and let the Skunks have the copy. But Mel's got the copy!*

He reached for his mobile phone and was about to call Mel when he remembered that the Skunks might have bugged that as well as the one in the house. He would have to run to Mel's. Quickly he pulled off his magician's coat and dashed downstairs into the empty front room. Within a moment the disc was out of the curtain hem and in his hand. He looked at it carefully. The small silver square on the top was clear. Alongside, handwritten in pen, were the letters 'BD3'.

We really can't let the Skunks have this. We can give them the copy and they won't know the difference!

In a moment the disc was safely stored inside his small backpack. He then moved into the hall and put his head around the living-room door.

'Just going into the shed, Mum. One of our props needs repairing and I have to time the music to the first part of the show again.'

Mrs Piper jumped when he spoke. 'Sam, you frightened me then! Well, don't be long. It's getting late. You know you spend too long in there ...'

Minutes later Sam was pounding down the streets. Perhaps he should have told his mother he was going out for a run, just in case she appeared at the door of the shed. But in another few minutes he was standing outside Mel's house. He waited a moment to recover his breath before he rang the doorbell. Mrs Eastwood answered the door.

'Sam! Good grief, have you run all the way? What are you doing here at this time of night?'

He reached inside his backpack, and brought out an illusionist's book.

'Sorry, Mrs Eastwood, but Mel said she wanted to look at this tonight before we meet for a practice tomorrow. Can I go up and give it to her? We might need to change part of the show and there may be ideas in here.'

Jeanette waved him inside. 'She's in her room. Go on up.'

'Thanks, I shan't be long!'

Within a few minutes Sam had shown Mel the silver square on the top of the original disc and had persuaded her of the need to make the swap. Then, just a few minutes later, he bid her goodnight with a satisfied grin and scampered downstairs, calling 'cheerio' to Mel's mum over his shoulder, before pounding the streets back to his house.

As he walked through the door, Sam checked where his mother was, then secreted the disc in the curtain again. His mother had hardly moved a muscle in the time he had been at Mel's house, just watched TV in a tired trance. He went to sit with her for a few minutes before going to bed. Then, as he climbed the stairs, he pictured Uncle Jack's angry face and wondered whether he should have left everything to MI21.

Meanwhile, at Skunk Headquarters, Mad Skunk Skuda was about to have visitors. Mad Skunk Silas and Mad Skunk Bulldog marched along the corridors and through the high-security doors to a semi-curtained bay in the medical wing, where Skuda was recovering from his fall. Silas moved the curtains aside and stood at the end of the bed, smirking.

'Feeling any better, Skuda? We heard that most of the bruising was to your, er, posterior. Nasty. It's amazing what damage a couple of schoolkids can do.'

'Indeed. Thank you, Silas. Nice of you to drop by. Have you brought any grapes?' said Skuda, gritting his teeth.

He was sitting propped up on the bed, his head heavily bandaged, with only one eye showing. Under his pyjamas Silas and Bulldog could see the shape of the heavy strapping that supported the three broken ribs and bruised torso. His left arm was held against his body by a sling, to ease the pain of his broken collarbone, and a thick, hot-looking collar encased his bruised and twisted neck.

Silas smiled sweetly. It wasn't often he could bait his main rival in the Mad Skunks, and he was determined to make the most of the opportunity.

'It's just as well they didn't send any real MI21 agents to rescue their disc, if this is what a couple of kids can do! Perhaps we need to introduce some special training. How about a course called Stealing Candy From a Baby?' Silas patted Skuda on the head in a deliberately patronizing way and Bulldog sniggered.

Skuda took a deep breath, then shouted for Tania, his nurse, to bring him some water. He was determined to stay calm, but inside he was boiling with rage. How dare they! He'd show them. He'd teach Silas and

Bulldog to mock him. Him! Mad Skunk Skuda. Where was that wretched nurse? (Unfortunately, Skuda had forgotten that it was Saturday, her day off, so help would not come from that direction.)

'You know nothing, Silas. Strutting about like some little dictator, trying to impress me. Well, it won't work! We need that disc, and at least I had a go at getting it, unlike some I could mention.'

Silas pulled a folded sheet of paper from his pocket. 'There are other ways of getting things, you know,' he said smugly. 'Ways that aren't quite as . . . drastic as yours.'

Skuda struggled to take the paper, but Silas waved it temptingly just out of reach.

'This is the transcript of a telephone call from the boy, Sam, to Jack Sanders. Sam is obviously frightened and wants shot of the disc. He pleads with Sanders to pick it up. The two kids then tell Sanders exactly where it is hidden – in a curtain hem in the boy's front room! We'll pick it up later, when they're all asleep! You see, Skuda, James Bond heroics just aren't necessary in today's world.'

Silas and Bulldog smirked at each other and left the bay.

Skuda stared at the ceiling, fuming. *Just wait*, he said to himself. *I'll show you what Mad Skunk Skuda does to people who cross him. I'll get even. And as for those kids* ... For the next five minutes he allowed himself the pleasure of imagining a variety of horrible fates for Mel and Sam.

Sunday morning

In Montrose Drive, during the early hours of Sunday morning, a black van drove silently along the street and stopped just short of Sam's house. Without a sound, rear and passenger doors opened and shadowy figures emerged then seemed almost to vanish as they made their way to the front gate of number 35. Within seconds they had surrounded the house, whilst two Skunk Stealth Troopers quietly moved to the side door.

A short distance away, unbeknown to the Mad Skunks, two MI21 agents lay hidden in the shadows under a hedge across the street. They had been there for nearly three hours and their legs had gone to sleep from remaining in the same position.

Using night-vision binoculars they witnessed and recorded the Skunk unit easily break in through a side door, using a key they had manufactured from information gathered on their last visit.

At 2.08 a.m. the Skunks had entered the house. At 2.10 a.m. they swiftly left by the same means except that one Skunk's exit wasn't as silent as his entry. He left the house clutching his arm and neck and bounced against the gate as he stepped out on to the pavement.

For the first time the hidden agents heard spoken words.

'What the hell was that in there?'

'Just a cat.'

'A cat? You're joking. They've got a fully grown man-eating leopard in there!'

'Must have been that cat I heard about last week. Chewed up one of our guys real bad.'

'Look at the state of my arm! I should have been warned. I'm gonna bleed all over the place! I'll sue someone for this!'

'Will you two shut up!' hissed another. 'We've got the disc, now let's go!'

The Skunk unit piled back into their large black van which started moving off before the last door had closed.

The M121 agents breathed a sigh of relief, and not just because they could now stretch their legs. 'Right, time to phone for back-up. They've got some trailing to do.'

However, there came the sounds of other vehicles. The agents kept their heads down and within seconds a RapidoPost van drove past them, followed by a second. The first soon overtook the black van; the second stayed behind.

They were now travelling in convoy, moving north out of Whitewater. In 30 minutes they would stop and transfer the disc to a van at a RapidoPost depot, and at a given signal at least eight RapidoPost vans would emerge at the same time and travel in eight different directions, completely confusing MI21 and making pursuit impossible. They would not be able to track the disc.

CHAPTER 11

Sunday late morning

ILAS AND BULLDOG WERE BACK IN THE hospital wing, looking triumphant. They had even more to gloat over now. Silas approached Skuda's bed with a spring in his step.

'I just thought you'd like to know that we've got the disc,' Silas said brightly. 'I can't imagine how your lot missed it. Still, at least we've got it now. Brains not brawn, Skuda, that's what's needed.'

Skuda shuddered with dislike. 'It was those wretched kids,' he hissed. 'Those kids are good, Silas. They're not ordinary kids. They've got weird skills and they've had specific training ...'

'Oh, that's how they knocked you out of the helicopter, is it?' chuckled Silas. 'Their weird skills and special training ... as entertainers in old-folks' homes!'

Mad Skunk Skuda felt a flush of irritation fill his cheeks. He started to cough as he was reminded of his embarrassment.

'You've had better days, Skuda,' continued Silas with a malicious grin. 'Thrown out of a helicopter by two kids . . . and lost your trousers!' Silas and Bulldog began to laugh hysterically.

Skuda scowled, and decided to change the subject. He lay back against his pillow. 'Well, Silas, what I want to know is what's so special about this disc? Why would details about shipments or whatever be transferred that way? Why weren't they sent in code through the post or the Internet or scrambled through the phone. Why did MI21 put them on a disc that could so easily get lost or stolen? It sounds suspicious to me.'

Silas was too busy wiping away tears of laughter to reply, so Bulldog took over. 'There is something else on the disc: highly sensitive information from one of our double agents working within MI21; information that could virtually destroy the whole of that government organization! It will take them years to recover. They don't know that information is on the disc. They think they are feeding us details about a shipment to Hull, but in fact there's another shipment of stolen goods coming from Kent that's worth a small fortune, and we know the date, time, method of transport, security cover, everything! It's just brilliant! MI21 try to destroy us and we end up attacking them!'

'Why haven't I been in on this?' asked Skuda angrily.

'We run a busy organization, Skuda. We all have our own sections to run. This wasn't one of yours,' replied Bulldog.

Skuda leaned forward, spluttering. 'I should have been told! I'm on an equal footing to you. I represent one third of this entire empire. I'm one of the founder members!'

'Some founder member!' grinned Silas. 'It was you who failed to find the disc and got knocked out of a helicopter by a pair of kids. You're a joke!'

With this parting shot Silas turned on his heels and made towards the ward exit, Bulldog following close behind.

They walked towards the elevator to the lower levels. In the silence of the enclosed lift Silas pressed the button that gave him access to an underground area known as Unit 6. As the lift stopped and the bell pinged, Bulldog tapped in his security code.

The doors opened and they stepped out into an enormous factory, divided into different sections with further doorways leading off to distant units. As you know, RapidoPost is the artificial front of the Skunk Empire, and is run as a profitable company, but here, in Unit 6, lay the beating heart of the Mad Skunk Empire.

Here, in all its sprawling splendour was the developing beast of an illicit 'copying' organization. Here, thousands of illegal copies were made of music CDs, computer CD-ROMS, T-shirts, sweatshirts, perfumes, cameras, watches, works of art . . . It was all going on here. The cash generated from these goods was virtually pure profit, with nothing going to the original designers. This was a mammoth enterprise, capable of generating billions of euros through worldwide sales.

Employees were paid well and told not to talk about their work outside. They understood this was for the well-being of the company and also because if they spoke about what they were doing to anyone they would lose their homes, possessions, children, dog and lavatory seat and be living in the sewer under their town's high street only to see daylight through a drain cover.

Conditions were made as pleasant as possible and the workforce had few reasons to moan about their jobs and endanger the organization. They had five weeks' holiday a year, an hour-long dinner break, and two other half-hour breaks in their eight-hour shifts. They had free medical cover, a company car, four free T-shirts and sweatshirts a month; free trainers for the family every six months; free perfume and aftershave every two months; a free CD of their own choice every month and a free 500-euro watch every year.

The workforce happily accepted all of the extras, on top of a rate of pay one and a half times the best other local rate. When compared with living in a sewer, with no house, child, dog or lavatory seat, employees quickly came to the conclusion that there really was no need to speak to anyone about their job, not even their partners. The majestic firm RapidoPost was indeed a fantastic organization to work for – as long as you kept quiet.

Silas and Bulldog spent an hour marching around the different factory areas and divisions, examining goods and packaging. They were particularly pleased with the CD pressing unit where 10,000 pirated copies of the top 50 albums were being produced every day.

As they came towards the end of their tour, Silas turned to Bulldog. 'We got the disc last night, but Skuda's right about one thing: those kids have given us too much of a runaround. They have to be warned to stay out of this game. We need to do something to really frighten them. Clearly, hanging out of a helicopter wasn't terrifying enough for these kids. We must do something that tells them not to meddle with us and also offers us a little bit of revenge for the amount of time we've spent chasing that blasted disc.'

That same morning, Sam was helping himself to breakfast when his tousle-haired mother staggered into the kitchen.

'Morning, Mum!'

'Ow, my head. I feel awful.' She flung open a cupboard to search for the aspirin.

'The disc has gone, Mum. They must have come in the night and taken it.'

'Oh, Sam, I hate the thought of people coming in here in the dead of night. I hope they didn't spray gas all around the place again. Perhaps that's why I feel so groggy.'

'Well, I feel all right. Aren't you pleased the disc has gone?'

'I suppose so, but the ruddy thing shouldn't have been here to start with. Never mind, it's gone now. Perhaps we can just get on with our lives and they'll all leave us alone, including that Uncle Jack and his MI21 cronies.'

Sam moved the chopping board on to the kitchen unit. 'Do you want some toast, Mum?' he asked, cutting himself a slice of bread from his loaf.

'Yes, I think I will . . . ' She was stopped by a thump that seemed to come from the front room. Sam and his mother looked at each other. Sam put down the knife and turned towards the noise as they heard yet another thump from the front room. Carefully they both moved out of the kitchen towards the room where Sam had secreted the disc.

As soon as they entered, Sam's mum spotted the

hem of one of the curtains hanging down at one end.

'Oh, look what they've done!' She moved forwards and picked up the lower half of the curtain. 'Just look at that!'

'Well, you didn't expect them to sew it back up, did you?'

'Sam!'

'Mum, they're a criminal gang. They're into drugs, smuggling, counterfeiting and even the slave trade, I'm told. You don't really expect them to carry a curtain repairer around with them in the back of a van, do you?'

'But look at this . . .'

Sam put on another voice, 'Dangerous mission, Boss, better send in The Curtain Repairer!'

'Sam!'

At that moment there was a thump and a scratch from behind the cupboard door, which had been wedged shut with a dining-room chair.

'It's Puffin! They've shut him in!'

Sam's mother put a hand on his arm. 'Sam, look at the top of the unit. What are those horrible messy marks all over it?' Her eyes were drawn to the wall, where dark-red smears ended in the clearly identifiable shape of a handprint.

'Is that blood? Just look at the mess!'

'If Puffin is in the cupboard, then that will definitely be blood on the wall. He must have made mincemeat of the intruders last night.'

'I think you had better think about letting your cat out. Goodness knows what damage he's done in there.'

'He's not my cat!'

'Well, he's not mine either! There'll be nothing left in the cupboard, Sam. He will have recycled everything into shredded wheat. Go and pull the chair away.'

'You pull the chair away! He'll be out of that cupboard and straight at your face, thinking you're the intruder from last night.'

Eventually they decided to hold the cupboard door closed with a broom handle while they pulled the chair away together. Then they would both run out of the room as fast as possible and leave Puffin to push the door open himself. They knew what mood he would be in, so there was no point in staying around to ask if he wanted any breakfast.

Within ten seconds of leaving the room Sam and his mother heard the sound of the cupboard door being violently slammed open and Puffin, a spitting ball of venomous anger, clawing his way back into the world. The clangs, bangs, rips and screeches tore through the stillness of the kitchen.

'You'll have to do something about that cat!' said Mrs Piper.

'He's not mine! He followed *you* home, Mum. *You* gave him something to drink and eat. *You* called me to see him. *You* let him stay that first night. He's *yours*, Mum! *You* even gave him the ridiculous name of Puffin!'

'But I did it for you. I thought you wanted a pet.'

'I did. I wanted a dog, not a spitting, slicing, fur-ball from some alien movie.'

When the sounds from the front room had died down and they had both finished crunching Sam's delicious granary toast Sam explained that he was hoping to spend the day practising for the show with Mel. They hadn't really put much thought into it, as they had been otherwise engaged over the last busy week. But they had to do as much as possible today to make sure the programme was fully organized and that everything was working properly.

Mrs Piper, pleased that Sam was going to occupy himself with normal activities for the day, declared that her head was a little better and that a good shower was what she needed. She left Sam in the kitchen washing up and swished her way out of the room. Halfway up the stairs she remembered something, stopped and leaned over the banister. 'Sam, you'll have to get in touch with Uncle Jack today. Tell him the disc has gone and that there's blood over the cupboard and the wall. They'd better clean it up as it's all their fault. And anyway, there might be DNA traces they'd want to follow up. Have you got that, Sam?'

'Yes, Mum,' Sam replied, even though he hadn't really heard; he was trying to think what should come second and third in their act on Saturday.

It was just before 10.30 when Sam opened the front door to Mel. Her mother followed her in with a 'Good morning, Sam. Hope you have a good practice today. I need to have a word with your mother. Is she in?'
'She's in the front room. I think she's fixing the hem on the curtain.'
'Right, bye then, you two. I'll pick you up this afternoon, Mel. About 4.00?'
Mel had already disappeared through the kitchen door. She called back over her shoulder, 'Yes, please, Mum. I'll give you a call if we need more time. Bye!'
Mel and Sam dashed out of the back of the house, across the patio and into the Pipers' large wooden shed. Mr Piper had erected it the year before. Originally he had just wanted to put up a garden shed, for tools and potting compost, but Sam had talked him into making it much larger so he and Mel would have some space to practise in and keep their props.

To start with the shed had seemed huge and the children had plenty of space. But now the amount of equipment they had was growing in quantity and volume. Shelving on one wall held the smaller items – pieces of rope, wands, juggling balls and bunches of flowers – and the larger pieces leaned against the far end of the shed. Mr Piper had some of his own tools and equipment on narrower shelves on the other side. This left only one long side free, and the children used that as their practice area.

At just over six metres long their shed was larger than average, but it was by no means big enough for them to run through the whole show. So, for one evening every month, they booked the village hall on the outskirts of Whitewater in order to run through the show's entire programme. They had the village hall booked for this Tuesday evening for three hours.

Mel and Sam looked around at all the equipment, wondering where to start.

'It's a two-parter for us this Saturday, Mel, so we're going to have to take loads of props with us. We'll have to load up the van as soon as we can.'

'OK. But I feel a bit out of practice. It seems like years since we did the last one, and then we've got two others to do before we break up for the summer. That's only five weeks away!'

'Well, we've got to get the programme sorted out today. We'll practise each trick and then have a proper run-through on Tuesday.'

'Do you know what's happening on Saturday? Are we on first?'

'Mum says we are, though she doesn't know what

time we'll finish, mainly because of the break. You know what it's like, the old folk just go on for ages . . . tea, biscuits, cake, chat, raffle . . . But the idea is, we do our bit, then there's a singer and his keyboard player to finish off the first half. After that there'll be the break and, depending on how long that is, the second half should start at 8.45, 9.00 at the latest.'

They spent nearly an hour considering the content of the programme.

'Sam, I think I can do the throwing the frisbees in Rundale Hall. They usually leave quite a wide central aisle. I can put three hoops along it and throw from the stage. I'll get them to land in the hoops, no problem.'

'What if one of the old dears might want to stand up and catch one, and throw it back . . . ?'

'Or knock one flying with a walking stick! No, I think it'll be OK. That bit will only take a minute, so if there's no aisle we'll leave it out!'

'Well, you could always do your "power of the mind" trick instead.'

Sam smiled at Mel. He understood that she got frustrated because though she really wanted to demonstrate her superb throwing skills there was seldom enough room. She loved it when they could perform at an outdoor event where there was plenty of space.

It was difficult with a two-part performance as you

had to have two impressive starts and two spectacular endings. They had just started talking about the second half when the shed door burst open and in jumped Mr Piper, Sam's dad. His arms were wide open and he had a big grin on his face. 'Da-dar!' he shouted in a big, theatrical way, and started doing a jig around the floor. 'Hello, Mel! Hi, Sam!'

Sam ran over and flung his arms around him.

'Dad, what are you doing here? Why have you come so early?'

'Oh, my Monday and Tuesday conference was cancelled, so I thought I would come straight home, instead of spending time in the . . . er . . . office! However, I've still got to go off later in the week, probably on Thursday.'

'So you're here until Thursday?'

'Yep! I'll help with the practice in the village hall, but I'm afraid I won't be able to see the show on Saturday.'

Mr Piper could see the hurt in Sam's eyes. He had hardly seen any of the children's shows; he felt very guilty about it but they hardly ever coincided with his days off.

'I'm sorry, Sam, but you know how it is. I'll do what I can to help you with the show before I go, but for now I'll leave you two to get on. See you later,' and with a cheery wave he was gone.

Mel and Sam started to think about an outline for the second half of the performance. Mel tried out a few of the characters she wanted to impersonate. They checked out Sam's trick guillotine – they still got a laugh out of using an old bucket to catch the head of the poor 'volunteer' – and discussed some of Sam's illusionist tricks.

But after the first run through they both felt that it was time to think about a new finale to their act. They wanted something new.

It was just after 3.00 p.m. when Mr Piper came back into the shed, bearing welcome supplies of tea and chocolate biscuits, to see how they were getting on. The children took the opportunity to show him the model that Sam had created. They explained about the box on castors and how it had a secret bottom to it, just wide enough for someone to hide in, complete with a variety of objects, like bunches of paper flowers. They explained that it could have a trap door at the back, and how this would open when the sides of the box were up and the lid placed on top. Someone could slide through the gap, the trap door would be closed, the lid taken off, the hinged sides of the box lowered to the floor, and Mel or Sam would appear to have vanished.

Sam's dad was very impressed with the model.

'Well, it doesn't look too difficult to construct. I'll go and pick up the materials tomorrow. I'll get started over the next few days, but I don't think I'll be able to get it finished before I go on Thursday.'

'Yeah, we know that, Dad. This is brilliant! When it's done we'll do all the painting and then we'll need quite a lot of practice before we can put it in the show. Maybe we can unveil it at the school performance, just before we break up for the summer holidays?'

'OK, I'll try and do a bit more next week and finish it off.' Mr Piper looked at both of the children and became serious for a moment. 'Mum's been telling me about what's been happening over the last few days. I just can't believe it. I must say you're incredibly brave kids. I don't know how I would have coped.'

Sam looked at Mel. *He doesn't know the half of it!*

'Mum thinks some of the problem might be because I don't spend enough time with you.'

'It's not that, Dad!'

'Well, anyway, perhaps she's right, but I'm just away so much these days. So I'll be more than happy to help construct this illusionist's contraption. And,' he said with a smile, 'it'll give me an excuse not to paint the bedroom that your mum's on about!'

Both children laughed. Sam went over to give his father a hug. 'Thanks, Dad!'

Suddenly Mel's face dropped; she wished that her

own father would walk in through the shed door and lend a hand. She could think of nothing better than seeing him helping Mr Piper to build some equipment for the show. She didn't think he'd ever even seen the shed. Then she caught Sam looking her way. She smiled quickly and pushed the thought from her head – things *were* getting better, after all. The disc had gone and they'd had a great day practising for the show . . . and she was going out with *her* dad tomorrow. The only way was up!

Far away in Bay 3, Skunk Headquarters, Mad Skunk Skuda stared up at the ceiling. Tomorrow he should feel fit enough to move. Then he would find out more about that stupid disc. He'd find out just what this convoy was all about and he'd take control. Ha! He'd get even with Silas for laughing at him.

He had designed most of this complex and he knew exactly how to find out what was going on – and no one would know how he did it. Pay-back time was coming.

Tania at the desk outside heard his demented laugh over the intercom. She didn't know what he was laughing at but it sent a shiver down her spine and she felt the small scar on the side of her mouth tighten . . .

CHAPTER 12

Digital discoveries

ONDAY MORNINGS ALWAYS STARTED with excited chatter by the school gates as children recounted various events, happenings, parties, visits and disasters that had happened in a variety of households over the weekend.

Mel and Sam looked at each other across the playground. They knew they could easily produce a brilliant story. Mel winked at Sam. It was frustrating being a secret agent sometimes.

Just before school started, Mel had a chance to catch Sam alone.

'I looked at the disc again last night. You know there were those strange files that had loads of coded messages in them?'

'Yes, the list of ten websites – garden sheds, dogs

on flowerpots and the like ... '

'Yes, well, I explored some of the sites but they were all completely boring. Then I went on to a search engine and tried to locate a few of the others. I couldn't find any. Not even the one called Garden Sheds I Love. Whoever made these websites doesn't want anyone to look at them.'

'But that's daft. What's the point of making a website if you don't want anyone to look at it?'

'Exactly. But then, just as Mum told me to get off the Internet and go to bed, I pulled the cursor across a picture of a shed called a Sun King "K", and just by chance it landed on the picture of a poppy in the bottom left-hand corner. Lo and behold, a little box came up with the words "Go Friday" and another website address. So then I got interested, but of course, right on cue Mum walked in and I had to close it all down and go to bed. I can't work on it tonight, I'm going out with Dad. Can you take another look, Sam? I think you may be right about that silver square. There could even be something on there that Uncle Jack doesn't know about!'

'Oh, Mel, I'm sure the entire Mizi organization knows exactly what they are doing and what is on the disc. I feel like a complete twit for swapping the discs the other night.'

'Sam, please ... '

'OK, you might be right, I'll pick it up on the way home.'

They travelled the long way round to Mel's house, even though they both knew that the Mad Skunks were fully aware of where they lived.

When they arrived at Mel's house they carefully extracted the computer disc from beneath the floorboard in her room, then Sam placed it in his backpack, said his goodbyes and left Mel to get ready for a night out with her dad.

Sam was determined to spend at least two hours researching the contents of the disc that evening, so when he got home he did his homework straight away, and then he went up to the computer in the study. He had just managed to trawl through the contents of the disc, refreshing his memory as to what was there, when he heard his mother come in from work, shouting, 'Hello, Sam' at the top of her voice and asking him to tidy his school stuff away. He switched off the computer and hid the disc ready for more exploration after dinner.

At 6.30 he sat down with his parents for a dish of lasagne.

'How's the design for the illusionist's box coming on, Dad?'

'I've made a great start, Sam. In fact, I've been

working on it all day. I managed to sketch things out this morning and then went to town to buy all the materials. I thought you would have come out to see it when you came home.'

'Sorry, Dad. I had to start my homework as soon as I got in. I've got a load to do.'

'Have you got more to do tonight? You're not going on the Internet are you?' asked his mother.

'Yes, Mum, a little bit. And I've got a disk from school. They want to see if we can locate the correct information on it. Test our research skills. Stuff like that!'

'How long will that take you?' asked Mr Piper.

'I dunno. Couple of hours, I expect.'

'Well, I think they give you too much homework at that place.'

Sam's mum coughed. 'Excuse me, what do you know? You're hardly ever here. You don't know how much he gets. I don't think they give them enough homework. He only comes home with a piece a week. I'm sure they should have more than that!'

'Mum . . . ' Sam had heard this often enough. As far as he was concerned he was getting just the right amount – virtually nil – and he didn't want his mother going down to the school asking for more!

When the meal had finished, Sam badgered his father to show him how much he had done on the illusionist box. As the pair of them stepped through the shed door Sam's jaw fell wide open, for there in the middle of the floor sat the lower part of the box, complete with trap door in the base. Around it, loose on the floor were the side panels. His father explained that everything had gone together like a dream and that that evening he hoped to put on the sides and attach the wheels underneath the box.

All other thoughts drifted away as Sam examined the construction.

'This is great, Dad. I didn't think you would have done so much.'

'Nor me. But it's all going so well that it should be finished tomorrow.'

'Tomorrow?' Sam could hardly believe what he had heard.

'Just got to make the lid, then all the hard work's done. I'll get all the edges smoothed off and a coat of primer paint put on by the time you escape from school.'

Sam smiled up at his father. 'Thanks, Dad.'

'Pleasure, Sam. Now let's see if you can get in through that trap door.'

Within a minute Sam was inside and had pulled the door shut.

'It's dark in here!'

'Yes, I've already drilled air holes so there's a little

light down there, but I'll have a bulb and battery attached inside by Wednesday.'

'I think there's plenty of space in here for keeping all sorts of things.' Sam opened the door, pulling himself into a sitting position. 'Then I'll be able to put out all manner of objects on to this platform while the sides are up.'

He pretended to place objects around him before sliding back underneath and closing the trap door.

His father smiled, pleased that he was able to do something to help with the Spectacular Show and take Sam's mind off the dangerous world of MI21.

Sam, however, was about to be drawn even closer.

While Mel was enjoying herself at the cinema with her father, and a large bucket of popcorn, Sam was totally absorbed in a screen of his own.

After an unsuccessful half an hour of trying to crack the two pages of coded messages on the Word document, Sam gave up. There was no way he could decipher the code of symbols, letters and numbers. He just hoped that the Skunks had the equipment to break the code and understand the message.

He recalled how angry Uncle Jack had appeared to be when he believed that the original disc had been nailed to the gatepost. The Mad Skunks were supposed to receive this message. Uncle Jack had said it was leading them to a supposedly valuable consignment of goods arriving in Hull. It was all a carefully constructed plan to feed false information to the Mad Skunk Smuggling Unit. Skunk agents would meet the consignment, but when they collected the container in Hull they would be pounced upon and arrested by MI21 agents and the police.

Sam assumed that the pages of gobbledegook gave times, sailings, container numbers and passwords. *But what if it isn't that?* thought Sam. *What if the information isn't that list of coded words, but is hidden somewhere else?* He then remembered what Mel had said about a website.

The rest of the disc looked as if it was full of very ordinary files, rather like those anyone might have at home. Under Publisher there were two available files. One of these had coded messages; they were short, just words or phrases, but Sam was unable to understand anything. The other file seemed to have only fifteen blank pages on it, as if someone had set the file up and then forgotten to write anything. There was an Excel folder with just one file in it, but this just had a list of figures in thousands, totalled at the bottom. It didn't seem to be a very professional way of passing highly secretive information on to anybody.

Elsewhere on the disc he found two digital photographs. One showed a Yorkshire terrier sitting on a large upturned flowerpot. There was nothing remarkable about this. It was just someone's pet. The other showed a couple with their arms around each other, standing outside a cottage with a fine orange, red and yellow sunset behind them. In the distance, in silhouette, was a column set on top of a rocky ridge. Both of these images looked like family photographs that had mistakenly been left on the disc.

This left the list of ten websites on another Word file. Sam printed out the list. He decided he would start with the one that Mel had already been exploring at home: Garden Sheds I Love. There were twelve pages consisting of garden sheds, summerhouses, tree houses, gazebos and even dog kennels. The pages looked completely and utterly boring.

He eventually found the 'Sun King' summerhouse range she had mentioned. There were three variations. Mel had told him to have a look at the photo attached to the Sun King 'K' model. He found the poppies growing in the grass beside an upturned flowerpot, in the corner of the photo. He passed the mouse pointer across that part of the image. Just as Mel had said, the words 'Go Friday' popped up in a box, complete with another website address.

Sam clicked on the address, but nothing happened. It wasn't connected by a hyperlink. He tried typing it out in the address bar and entering it. In a moment he arrived at a single-page website. The site seemed to be a huge montage of pictures of cats and dogs. As the mouse pointer moved across the images, link boxes with further website addresses appeared. Sam clicked on a photograph of a Dalmatian and was transferred to a complex site with nothing on it but information on that breed. He returned to the original single-page site and clicked randomly on a few boxes. He spent 20 minutes exploring several more websites but could find nothing more sinister than a history of cats and their relationship with humans; the most popular breeds of dogs over the last 25 years; and big cats and why they are so endangered.

Feeling frustrated he returned to the Sun King "K" page. He carefully moved the pointer over the picture. No other information boxes came up, just the one that Mel had found accidentally. He returned once more to the poppies. The box came up. He moved the pointer away. The box disappeared. He moved it back.

'It's not the poppies that have got the tag,' he said to himself. He stared straight at the image, moving the pointer back and forth. Then, in a blinding flash it came to him: *Upturned flowerpot . . . upturned flowerpot!* His whole body went clammy as he saw the possible link.

He minimized the Internet page and uploaded the two digital photographs, the sunset and the image of the Yorkshire terrier sitting on . . . an upturned flower-pot. *Yes!* He transferred both of them to a Word page and printed them out. Then he went back to the single Internet page with all the images of cats and dogs. He searched for a frustrating few minutes. He was worried he was wrong; that the dog's breed wasn't there. And then, at the very moment he was about to give up, he found it. A tiny image, squashed between the head of an Alsatian and a sabre-toothed tiger. It was a Yorkshire terrier. It even looked as if it was the same dog from the photo with the flowerpot.

Sam moved the pointer over the tiny image. He clicked on the website address in the box, but this one had no hyperlink. He had to type it all out into the address bar. The screen faded to a very basic single-page site. He'd found it:

```
          BENK 32 CONSIGNMENT
     FROM SOUTH KENT STORAGE FACILITY


Leaving June 11th, 5.45am
Five container trucks to travel in convoy
Single armed guard in each cab
Armed police escort: Front car with two
                     armed officers
                     Rear car with three
                     armed officers
```

ROUTE

Join M20 at Junction 13

M25, through Dartford Tunnel

M1

Stop at Topline Services: extra police and army on guard here, plus armoured car

Continue north: M1, A1(M),

Hijack points: Suggest either J37 for Penny Whistle site or

continue to the Races site for 'Operation Flowerpot'

Crates/containers:

27 European Antiques

34 Works of Art

 9 Large framed classic paintings

11 BC Antiquity pieces

12 Statues

 5 Jewellery

 1 Cut/Polished stone

 1 Uncut stone

 3 Gold and other precious metals

 2 Collections of rare postage stamps

 2 Collections of rare coins

17 Rare animal skins

11 Dried endangered animal parts for medicines

 8 Dried tiger components

```
 6  Ivory, cut and uncut
 2  Rare birds' eggs collection
41  Drugs of various descriptions
23  Guns, assault rifles etc. (No explosive
    ammunition on board)
14  Other weapons, knives, swords etc.
```

Sam sat staring at the screen. His mouth was slightly open. Was this really what the Mad Skunks were to be told? Uncle Jack had mentioned a consignment. But he said that was coming in to Hull, not being stored in Kent, and that MI21 was hoping to catch about half a dozen Skunks using this ploy. This consignment from Kent was a great convoy of five trucks with an army and police escort. There was no way a single Mad Skunk unit would be able to hijack that lot. Five massive trucks of what seemed to be illegal goods: art; jewels; stamps and coins; endangered animal parts; drugs and weaponry. It must be important for the police and army to be involved in the convoy. It must be worth a fortune!

He then remembered the Excel folder on the disc. That had a list of figures on it. Figures in the thousands. He loaded up Excel and opened the file in the folder. A simple list of numbers came up. At the top, the title stated 'Estimated Value'. There were 19 sets of figures. The figures were in millions. If the 19 numbers had any connection with the 19 categories in the consignment then the total value of the convoy was a staggering £138, 654, 000.

Sam was shaking with the excitement of his discovery. He stood up and walked in and out of his bedroom with his hand on his head. Then he decided to have a break and go downstairs to get a drink of lemonade. As he entered the kitchen he heard a spitting sound: Puffin's pre-attack warning.

'Nice to see you, too, Puffin.'

The creature clawed the air and spat furiously at him.

Sam turned and yelled through the door, 'Mum, the cat wants feeding!'

To the sharks! he thought, and retreated to the safety of the hallway.

He'd have to have a glass of water from the bathroom instead of lemonade. He poked his head round the living-room door.

'I'm just finishing on the computer, Mum.'

Mrs Piper looked up from the TV and smiled sleepily. 'Well, don't be too long or you'll be too tired for school in the morning.'

She always said something like that, even though he could cope very well with staying up late and getting up for school.

'OK, Mum. Shan't be too long now.'

Back on the computer he was completely focused. He now knew how the system worked from the dog on the upturned flowerpot. Next he intended to apply the same principle to the picture of the couple outside the cottage and look for the main elements of that photo in the other websites.

It was at 9.20, with bleary eyes and drooping eyelids, that he made the breakthrough. On a 'Crabs at the Seaside' site there was an image of a crab on the edge of a pool, and behind it was an almost identical sunset to the one in the photo of the couple outside the cottage. Sam carefully ran the mouse over every tiny part of the glorious blend of yellows, oranges and reds.

Suddenly, on the edge of a tiny cloud, a box with the words 'Who Built This?' popped up with a website address. As with the previous photograph, this wasn't linked. Sam typed in the address and was given a montage page of what seemed to be a hundred tall structures from all around the world. Again, all of these were hyperlinked to legitimate websites. All except a tiny one that nestled, virtually hidden, between the image of Christ the Redeemer in Rio de Janeiro and Nelson's Column in London. This was the image of the column in the photograph. It had taken him several minutes to find what he knew would be a small image. But there it was, complete with a website address.

With trembling hands Sam typed this into the address bar and was immediately transferred to a site containing a list of names. Alongside each one was a title. Underneath he was able to find a telephone number, an address and the names of partners and children. On the third line was a date of birth, place of birth and bank account number. Sam's eyes read the first line of the document:

MI21: WHO'S WHO

His pupils danced up and down the page. With a faltering heartbeat his eyes settled on the third name down:

JACK SANDERS: European Director of Operations

This is not right! Something is very wrong! Why would MI21 send out details of all its top agents? There must be more than seventy people listed here.

Sam's mind was now in turmoil. He had to contact Uncle Jack. He had to tell him what he had found, as soon as possible. He moved his eyes away from the screen. He couldn't risk using the house phone, so he would have to use his mobile, even though it might also have been tampered with. Quickly he tapped in the direct line for MI21.

'Ministry of Information. How may I help you?'

'European Division, please.' Sam suddenly realized

he could be in trouble. Last week he and Mel forgot to ask for the new password. He might not get through to Uncle Jack.

'There is a fault on the line,' came back the coded message from the receptionist.

'We don't know the new password. The week before last it was "The Green Ones are Juicy", but we've been chased for a week and have not been updated.'

'I'm sorry. We no longer have green ones.'

'Look, is that Trudy Blueshoes? I know you no longer have green ones but I haven't been updated.'

'This is not Miss Blueshoes.'

'Please put me through. I have vital information!'

'But you could be anybody. I can't just put you through!'

'This is Samuel Piper. I need to speak to Jack Sanders, European Director of Operations. I work with Melanie Eastwood. She is his niece.'

'Sorry, but I have only been working here a few days. I need the right codes. I don't know you and I don't know Melanie Whatshername. Goodbye!'

With this he was cut off. Sam sat staring at the phone for a few moments before his eyes darted back to Uncle Jack's name and details on the screen. Dare he use that telephone number? At least he would be able to find out if the information on the website was correct.

He tapped in the number and within a moment or two it was answered. It was Jack Sanders.

'Uncle Jack. This is Sam Piper. I've got vital information to give you.'

'Sam, how did you get this number? I don't remember giving it to you. All phone calls from you should be redirected via the Ministry of Information reception desk.'

'I haven't been given the updated password. There's somebody new at the desk and she doesn't know me.'

'But how did you get this number?'

'I'll explain in a moment. This is very important. Is the line secure? I have vital information that can't wait until tomorrow.'

'Well, my line's secure. What about your mobile? I'm assuming it is a mobile you're on.'

'Yes, it is a mobile, and I think it's secure, though it was in the house the day we had a visit from the Mad Skunks last week.'

'Then keep everything brief.' Uncle Jack's manner was a bit curt, as if he was annoyed that Sam had his number.

Sam quickly told him that he had just found his number on an Internet website. He had also seen his home address and his bank account details, plus those of at least 70 other MI21 agents. There was a spluttering sound on the other end of the line. As an example, Sam read out information about the Supreme Commander-in-Chief of MI21, Sir Warren Fitzpatrick, and a Sir William Duckdown who was apparently Head of Drug Surveillance and lived at number four in the same street as Jack.

Uncle Jack coughed in shock and amazement. Sam had to wait a few moments before Uncle Jack could compose himself sufficiently to reply.

'Good grief, Sam, I don't know where you got this information from, but don't say anything more. I can't get a scrambler connection on to your mobile, so there's no way to code your words.'

'Uncle Jack, there's more. I also have accurate details of a Benk 32 Consignment coming up from south Kent.'

'Holy mackerel, Sam! How do you know anything about this? That consignment is a top-secret project. It's moving millions of euros' worth of confiscated goods from the south-coast ports.'

'It's worth £138, 654, 000 to be exact, Uncle Jack.'

The spluttering cough restarted. Sam decided that Jack Sanders needed to give up smoking those revolting cigars.

'And I know the route it's taking and what's in each of its crates on the five trucks, and where it's stopping and details of its escort and . . . ' Sam held his breath, 'I think I've got two likely hijacking points.'

'Please, Sam . . . don't tell me any more on the phone. You're saying far too much! I need a clue as to how you have done this. Let me see. Give me a Mystic "R".'

Sam scrabbled for a pen and a piece of paper. A 'Mystic' could usually be created in moments using a simple phrase or sentence. It was a way of sending individual letters that, when put together, would create a particular word, or words, to provide the receiver with a clue. Sam wanted to send the word 'DISC'. In a 'Mystic' the receiver would look at the first letter of the first word, then the second letter of the second word, then the third letter of the third word and so on.

Sam struggled with the fourth letter, so he told Uncle Jack he would be sending him a Mystic 3R. This meant that after three words the fourth one would revert to the first letter. 'R' meant the phrase would have to be reversed on receipt.

Sam's message was, 'Clergy disbelieves pink dingo.'

Uncle Jack would reverse this to 'Dingo pink disbelieves clergy.' From this he would get the word DISC.

Sam waited in silence as Uncle Jack deciphered the code. When Jack spoke again he was deadly serious.

'Sam, I know it's very late, but I'm going to have to get up to Whitewater immediately. I'll have a helicopter bring me and a couple of agents up to a nearby field. We'll be met by a car and should be with you in about two and a half hours. Go to bed and get some sleep, but when we get there you must show us everything. Is that clear?'

Sam confirmed that it was.

'Now I want you to take this phone down to your mother.'

'My dad's here as well!'

'Good. Take it to them and I'll do the talking. They have to know that we'll be arriving after midnight. I don't think your mother will be very happy, but we have no choice. See you soon.'

Sam took his mobile downstairs and handed it to his mum. Then he retreated to the hallway for the second time that night, to avoid the embarrassment of hearing his mother shout at the MI21 Director of European Operations. She didn't though. It was very strange. He could hear her going 'Uh-huh, uh-huh,' but there were no raised voices.

When Mrs Piper had finished speaking to Uncle Jack she came out into the hallway. Sam waited for the volcano to explode, but instead she just handed over the phone, wagging her finger in resignation. 'I told you "No more missions", Samuel Piper. However, you must have very important information for MI21, so who am I to interfere with vital government business? Up to bed and try to get a little rest before they arrive. I just hope they don't wake the neighbours. Spies indeed, they can make more noise than a pair of battling dustcarts.' Then she turned and went back to her husband in the front room.

As Sam got into bed he didn't think he'd be able to fall asleep with so many things going round in his head, but when a gentle shake brought him back to consciousness, he realized he'd been dead to the world. He rubbed his eyes, and glanced at his bedside clock. It was 12.35.

For the next hour he talked to Uncle Jack and two other agents, sitting in his bedroom. Sam told them everything, not even hiding the fact that he and Mel had made a copy of the original disc, quoting the Agents' Handbook Rule 724: 'Always take any advantage to copy details and information. Photograph it, photo-copy it, record it, if you can.'

Jack Sanders nodded his approval. Sam showed them exactly how he had broken the code, remember-ing to add that it was Mel who first noticed something worthy of investigation. The three adults seemed very impressed with their work.

'Sam, you have both done very well. No, indeed, you have done excellently!'

Sam blushed, and then remembered something else he had wanted to tell them. 'I'm sure there's something else on the disc. Look, here.' He held the disc beneath his bedside light. Uncle Jack stepped forward and Sam showed him the letters BD3, then the small silvery square on the surface of the disc. In the centre was a very small dot.

'What do you think it is, Sam?' asked Uncle Jack.

'I'm not sure,' replied Sam, 'but I think it's some sort of computer chip. That's why we thought it would be a good idea to give the Skunks a copy of this disc, not the original.'

Uncle Jack nodded, then turned to his colleagues. They whispered for a short while and Sam couldn't make out the words. He felt a little uncomfortable. Finally Jack turned to him again.

'Sam, we haven't put the microdot on there. Somebody else has. It may be a ploy to throw us off the scent. Far more information can be held on a disc than a microdot. We don't have a team available at the moment to study this more closely, so we're going to let you keep the disc for a couple more days. You have already demonstrated impressive levels of intelligence and I'd like to see if you can find anything else on it. If you do it will be our gain. If you don't ... well, we won't have lost anything, will we?

'Of course, this whole matter needs investigating. Someone within MI21 has purposefully leaked this information to the Mad Skunks. We must have a double agent working within our ranks, high up in our management team. The information you have located about MI21 personnel is top secret. It could be very damaging to the organization. The Skunks now have that info. We will all have to change bank accounts, credit cards and telephone numbers before they can act. We'll have to post guards on everyone's front door. Many of us will have to move house.

'There's also the problem of the Benk 32 consignment delivery. I think it should still leave as originally planned. After all, the Skunks don't realize that we know they have the information. We may be able to use this to our advantage. I will call for a major meeting first thing tomorrow morning.' He looked at his watch and corrected himself, 'No, sorry, *this* morning!'

One of the agents hurriedly made a copy of the disc and gave the original back to Sam. Uncle Jack made for the bedroom door. Before he left he turned back to face Sam. 'Excellent work, Agent Piper,' he said, then he turned and was gone.

Sam got back into bed. Downstairs he could hear Uncle Jack apologizing for getting his parents out of bed, doors closing and lights being switched off. It was now almost 2.00 a.m. He turned off his bedside lamp, and almost immediately saw his parents outlined in the door frame. It was his father who spoke.

'Well done, Sam. Jack Sanders seems absolutely

delighted with the information you've given him. Apparently we aren't allowed to ask you what your meeting was all about, but "Well done" anyway. Goodnight, son.'

'Thanks, Dad.'

Then his mother spoke. 'You know what I'm going to say, don't you?'

'Yes, Mum. You're going to say, 'Well done, Sam, but ... no more missions!"

'How did you guess? Goodnight, Sam.'

Sam smiled in the dark. He closed his tired eyes. Things, people, computers, images, lists and websites whirled around in his head. But eventually, at 3.15 a.m., his mind finally drifted off into the soothing wash of a dream-filled sleep.

CHAPTER 13

Skuda's night

WHILE SAM WAS BEGINNING HIS DIGITAL discoveries, Skuda was planning a little adventure of his own. It was exactly 4.00 p.m. when nurse Tania came up to the control desk outside Bay 3 for her shift on ward duty. She examined Skuda's medical charts and flicked a channel over to the CCTV camera in the ward. Skuda lay there, exactly as he had the last time she had seen him. It was obviously too painful for him to move around much.

Tania decided that she must get Skuda up and make him do a few exercises. He may have cracked ribs and severe bruising, but he would need to get those legs moving and she needed him to become dependent on her. She would take him a walking frame during the evening.

But Skuda had other ideas.

It was 5.00 p.m. when Tania tapped in the security number one-seven-four-three on the ward door. Skuda had been waiting patiently. But now he complained to Tania of having nothing to do; there was nothing to watch on TV and nothing to listen to on the radio. He asked her to get hold of a portable CD player and a selection of the latest illegal copies from Unit 6, so he could test out the quality. Tania said she would see what she could do.

Skuda watched her with his functioning right eye as she performed her caring duties, checking him over, adjusting the strapping that supported his three broken ribs and changing a bandage on his thigh.

'You owe your life to a tree, Mr Skuda. Had you not landed in its tangle of branches and foliage you would be dead. A metre either side of it and there might have been nothing to break your fall. That tree saved your life. I hope you've said thank you to it.'

Skuda had done nothing of the sort. He cursed the tree – all trees – and the two kids who threw him out of the helicopter. But perhaps Tania was right. Perhaps the tree had saved him. *Beastly thing.*

Tania fussed a little with the bedclothes and then told him she would go and fetch his dinner. On her return, she spread out a large napkin to spare the bed-clothes from gravy dribbles and set the tray over his knees. As Skuda began to eat, gravy and bits of chewed vegetables dropped from his mouth.

What a state to be in, thought Tania, as she left him to finish his meal. *One of the most evil men in the world, and there he is creating a work of art in gravy on a napkin. I could sell it to the local gallery! Wait till I report back on this!*

Half an hour later she came in to clear up and brought in a walking frame to encourage Skuda to start moving his legs. He complained bitterly but it was obvious that she wasn't going to leave him in peace that evening until he had walked up and down the bay area at least four times. Skuda wanted her out of the way as soon as possible so he reluctantly obliged and began to tackle a series of difficult steps: each one sending a shock of pain right through his body.

Eventually Tania was satisfied with his progress and promised to leave him alone for the night. She left the walking frame at the base of the bed and went back to her desk outside.

Skuda waited just five minutes then carefully eased himself out of bed. As soon as he was on his feet he began to shuffle his way down to the bay door. He looked through the small window to check that everything was quiet out by the ward desk. Tania had her back to him and was pouring herself a glass of mineral water. Skuda watched to see what she would do. As soon as she placed the headphones of what appeared to be her CD player on her head and leaned back in a comfortable position in her swivel chair he punched his override code into the security combination lock on the door. Then, like an escaping Egyptian mummy, he shuffled out of the door towards a small storage room near the far end of the bay.

Now, though it was new security policy to change the access numbers on a regular basis, and nobody on the workforce could walk freely around the whole complex, this restriction had not applied to the three original Mad Skunks. They had had their own eight-digit master number, which could override any existing access number on any door.

Skuda was the only remaining original Mad Skunk. The others had been lost on missions, and neither Silas nor Bulldog had been around when the massive Mad Skunk complex was being designed and built. So, much of the information about the design of the complex had not been passed on. Skuda had kept this knowledge to himself to ensure that, at any given moment, he could access every department and check up on operations.

Inside the storage area there appeared to be only cleaning materials, sheets, spare curtains and the like. Most of these things were on shelves, except for the cardboard boxes of detergent stored on the floor. Skuda painfully got himself down on his hands and knees and moved two detergent boxes to one side. He then placed both hands on the skirting board and pushed sideways. The panel clicked and dropped forwards, exposing the wall behind. Skuda poked his fingers up inside the area where the skirting board had been and located a switch. He pressed down and immediately a digital security panel dropped into view.

Skuda poked his head out through the bottom of the door to check that Tania hadn't moved from her desk. As he finished tapping in his code number there came the sound of unlocking. Skuda flicked the switch again and the panel, on a small hydraulic arm, disappeared back up into the wall. He refitted the section of skirting board and returned the cardboard boxes to their original positions. Finally, he stood up, turned and gave a gentle push to the shelved wall beside him. The shelves swung out and Skuda stepped into a grey, poorly lit hallway. Despite his condition, this was not his first venture out of Bay 3 over the last couple of days. During his previous escapade, he had located an electric buggy, which was now waiting for him in the featureless corridor. He climbed slowly aboard and the buggy whirred into life.

On his journey into the depths of HQ he passed other doors leading off the corridor, each with their own identity number. These doors led to small service rooms and other cupboards throughout the complex. In all, there were twenty-five ways of gaining entry to the Skunk Empire from this dark, quiet corridor. Skuda was now the only one who knew about the huge underground labyrinth constructed by the original Skunks. This was his domain, and right now he was more than pleased that Silas knew nothing of its existence.

After passing several secret doors to Skunk work areas, Skuda found the door he wanted. He peered through its security peep-hole, and then tapped in his access number. He shuffled into a hallway with three doors. He stepped towards the door directly in front of him and into a room five metres square. This was his secret HQ control centre. There was a bank of twelve CCTV monitors on the facing wall, a central control desk, and three computers blinking and whirring away.

This secondary control centre, unbeknown to any-one in High Command, could easily override the primary control room known to the rest of management. From here Skuda could monitor everything that was happening within the Mad Skunk Empire, interact with the main computer and invalidate decisions made on the surface.

Skuda liked it down here. He enjoyed working with electrical gadgets and electronic equipment. Much of the hardware in this room he had installed himself.

He flicked a switch and watched Tania reading her book. As he did so he saw her look over her shoulder to glance at the CCTV monitor on her desk. Skuda then looked at the second monitor in his control room to check she was seeing what he wanted her to see. Yes, it was all going to plan. For what Tania was looking at was a looped video recording of the sleeping Skuda made over a day ago. Every time she glanced at the monitor she was looking at the same two minutes of digital recording.

For the next half an hour he checked all corners of Headquarters. He was happy with everything he saw except for the department that was meant to be investigating the MI21 disc. Most of these technicians were just sitting around chatting and laughing. Skuda needed to access their research from the mainframe computer in the control room but they weren't sending it to the central system quickly enough.

Skuda decided he needed a copy of the disc for himself. Given the speed at which this IT team were working he would easily be the first to crack the extra information on the disc.

Skuda smiled to himself. Silas and Bulldog would have quite a surprise when they found out just how much Skuda knew about what was going on at Headquarters. He'd make up for letting those two stupid Skunks steal a march on him before. 'Need to know basis' indeed.

Once he had the information from the disc they would have to take him a lot more seriously. With only the help of an MI21 mole, he, Mad Skunk Skuda, would crush Jack Sanders, Melanie Eastwood, Samuel Piper and MI21 European Operations for ever. Ha! That would teach Silas and Bulldog who was in charge.

Grinning maniacally to himself, Skuda made his way back through the secret corridors and returned to sit in the ward and set up his lap top. Now he must concentrate on breaking the code in the information he had copied from the IT research team's computer. He must succeed! The sale of the convoy's contents would help fund the secret Mad Skunk expansion plans under cover of RapidoPost.

Many honest businesses, legitimate organizations and individuals were now using this highly efficient delivery service. RapidoPost vans and trucks were a common sight in all areas of the country. Using this cover the Mad Skunk Empire would gradually take over the whole planet. And he, Mad Skunk Skuda would be the most admired Mad Skunk ever!

CHAPTER 14

Skuda gets even

THE MAD SKUNKS' HIGH COMMAND HAD assembled for a final meeting before the convoy hijack. Skuda was oozing satisfaction. He, and he alone, had discovered something no one else had dreamed of. The High Command had known that the disc contained details of an illegal goods convoy and some wonderfully destructive information about MI21 agents, but they had missed something...

Smugly, Skuda began: 'The disc you retrieved, Silas, is a copy. Our double agent, Skydive, planted an extra encoded microchip on the original disc, the one *you* failed to recover. The convoy has been booby-trapped by Skydive, in case our mission fails. If by some fluke MI21 manage to stop the hijack, Skunk Headquarters will set off the timer attached to bombs underneath the trucks. If we can't have the goods then neither can they! The only way the countdown can be stopped is by the original disc with the microchip being inserted in the correct equipment on one of the trucks. We do not need the disc to make the mission a success. However, as you all know, we fear MI21 agents may be working within our own organization. There remains the possibility that, after a successful hijack, this mole, this scumbag working somewhere in the Empire might press the destruct button just as we get the convoy to safety. Therefore we must have the disc with us on the mission. Skydive claims the disc has not arrived at MI21 Headquarters. So there is a strong possibility that those lousy, fruit-cake, scumbag kids still have it.'

Skuda watched with satisfaction as Silas's mouth dropped open. 'But, but, how did you find this out, Skuda?' he stammered.

'Sorry, Silas. Need to know basis only,' sneered Skuda. 'Anyway, the time has come to interrogate those lousy kids. We need to stop pussy-footing around and get on with the job.'

High Command liked what they heard and Skuda left the room to enthusiastic applause.

Silas, on the other hand, slunk out of the meeting with a face like thunder. He had missed the real disc, and somehow Skuda had managed to get a copy of it without leaving his hospital bed. Something wasn't right!

Back in his office, Skuda smiled to himself. 'Well, Silas, the boot's on the other foot now!'

That afternoon, after school, as the two children walked in through Sam's front door they couldn't believe their eyes. Someone had been in the house again! Papers and magazines were scattered over the floors; furniture had been moved and cushions tossed aside. In the front room the curtain that had held the secreted disc had been pulled off the wall and was now in a heap on the floor. In the kitchen things had been taken out of cupboards and thrown around. Cans and packets were everywhere, and the contents of a shredded bag of flour had been liberally distributed across the sink and drainer.

Running upstairs, Sam heard his father call his name. He burst into his parents' bedroom to discover Mr Piper sitting on the edge of his bed. Sam looked around at the open wardrobe doors and the clothing all over the floor. Mel stood behind him, open-mouthed.

'Dad? What happened? Who did this?'

His father held his head in his hands. 'I don't know. I just don't know!'

'But weren't you here? Didn't you hear anything? Did you see them?'

'No, I was working in the shed: on your new prop. I had been there a while and everything was going great. I thought I'd go and get some lunch, but when I stepped outside two police officers were standing in the garden. They said I was to accompany them to the police station to answer some questions. I tried to ask them what it was all about, but they just said that I'd find out when I got down there. They took me out through the side gate. I didn't even have time to check that the house was locked up. I went because I was worried something had happened to you or to your mother.'

'Well, where did they take you?'

'I don't know, but it wasn't a police station. The van I was in didn't have any windows, and when I got there they put a coat over my head and ran me through an open door. The next thing I knew I was in a bare room. An officer said somebody would be with me in a while, but nobody came. Then, nearly an hour later, I was bundled back into a van and dropped off in the middle of Whitewater.'

He looked around him, holding out his hands. 'And when I got back this is what I found. Looted and trashed.'

'Looted? What have they taken?'

'The computer and everything to do with it.'

'The computer?' Sam felt instantly deflated. That was the last thing they needed.

'Yes. And I haven't checked what else yet.'

'What about our stuff in the shed?'

'I haven't been in there.'

Sam dashed out towards the stairs. 'Come on, Mel. We'd better go and see if there's anything left.'

With this they almost tumbled down the steps in their race to the shed. When they got there they could see that things had been pulled off shelves and tossed to the floor. They stared at it all, and then slowly began putting a few things back in their places.

After a while, Sam's dad came in to join them. He walked to the centre of the room and righted the large box he had been working on.

'Ah, the paint's still tacky. That's probably why they left this alone. I painted it this morning. Look, there's a handprint right in the middle of the lid. I bet somebody got annoyed about having a dark-blue hand.'

Sam saw a print on the shelving frame. 'Look, he's left a mark here, too. The police would be interested in these. They might be able to match them with finger-prints in their criminal records.'

Mel ignored him, looking at the box. 'Wow, you've almost finished it!'

Murray Piper smiled. 'Yep. Just got some mystical signs to put on it, then it's ready for you two to use.'

'Wait a minute, Dad. What are all these slits all over the place?' Sam pointed at one of the many rectangular holes in one of the sides. 'Are they air holes?'

Mr Piper carefully took hold of the edges of the lid and pulled it off. The four sides stayed upright as they all peered inside.

'Look,' said Sam's dad, 'I've placed little guide runners inside.'

The children looked at a collection of slotted runners, each protruding about three centimetres from the sides into the space of the box.

'But what are they for?'

'Ah, now watch.' He put the lid back on and went searching among the items on the floor. Eventually he found what he was looking for. 'Good, they're still here. I only got them this morning.' With this he emptied the contents of a black bin bag. With a noisy clatter ten long swords fell to the floor. Immediately the children knew what they were for.

'And this is what you do.' Mr Piper picked up the nearest sword and inserted the tip into a slot on the side. He pushed it into the box. At the other end an open funnel shape caught the tip and guided it out through another slot on the opposite side.

'Wow, this is brilliant!' They each had a go, with Sam's dad showing them which slots were for inserting the blade and which for receiving. They stood and looked at the sword-peppered box.

'And all the time this is going on, one of you is safely out of the way in the base.'

'Brilliant, just brilliant!' exclaimed Mel.

'But, Dad, when the sides are down, won't the audience see the guiding blocks on the inside?'

'No, Sam. What I had planned to do this afternoon was to line the box with extra board on the inside. Each side will be rather thick, but I'll taper the edges so that the audience won't notice.'

Mel's face was a picture of happiness. 'Perhaps we could give it a go tonight?'

Mr Piper's smile slipped and he looked thoughtful. 'Tonight? Well, I'm not sure. I've got an awful lot of clearing up to do before Sam's mother comes in. She'll have a fit! And I'll have to contact the police and the insurance people. Anyway, don't you think you ought to be getting home? If this is anything to do with those Mad Skunks then they may well have been in your house too. Is anyone at home?'

Mel hadn't even considered this possibility.

'I think you'd better go home. Sam can go with you so you're not alone, and we can decide when to do a practice run after tea.'

Mel and Sam set off. At first they walked briskly, in silence, but suddenly Mel broke into a run. She was desperate to be home before her mother, in case the Skunks had been in.

When they burst through the front door of 18, Hillcrest Avenue it was obvious that, as they had suspected, the Eastwood family had had visitors again. Every room had been disturbed. It was clear that whoever had been in had been looking for something. Clothes, books, kitchen equipment and all manner of loose objects had been thrown about. Mel's mattress had been hauled off her bed. Her computer had also gone. They stood in silence, looking at the space it had once occupied.

'It must have been Skunks. They've done this to us.'

'But they've got the disc now. Why would they do this, Sam?'

'Perhaps it's because we tossed Skuda out of the helicopter? They want to get their own back.'

'Yeah, well they're certainly doing that.'

'But I think it's more likely that they have found out the disc they've got is only a copy. It all points towards there being something else that the Skunks need on that disc. Like the microdot. We don't have equipment to research that, but we do need more time to research those files and websites further.'

'What with?' asked Mel.

'What do you mean?'

'I mean, what with? We don't have a computer between us. They've even taken all our discs and games in their search for what they want.'

Sam stood deep in thought before replying with, 'Crumbs, we'll have to do it in school tomorrow.'

'We can't, remember Rule 724 section 7 in the Handbook?'

'Well, no, not really.'

'It goes something like, *'Never take prized and gathered information back into the field of conflict where it may be found and reclaimed by the opposing forces.'* We can't take it to school. We can't take it anywhere where we might be followed.'

'How do you remember all that stuff?'

'I don't know. I just do. Anyway, we had better check the real disc is still in its place.'

He pulled at her arm. 'Yes, but quietly. The rooms may be bugged again!'

Mel crouched down and levered up a small floorboard. Then she put her hand through the hole and reached up behind the skirting board. With a grin she pulled out the disc. Silently Sam put his thumbs up and she carefully returned the disc to its hiding place.

Suddenly the front door slammed and a horrified shout went up from Mrs Eastwood. She had discovered the mess inside. Mel and Sam hastily replaced the floorboard and ran to meet her.

CHAPTER 15

'When you're in, you're in.'

JACK SANDERS REPLACED THE RECEIVER WITH a sigh. He had just spent twenty minutes calming his sister and promising more MI21 protection for the Piper and Eastwood homes. Apparently they had been trashed. He stared out of the window of the MI21 building on the south coast. From here Jack Sanders could look between the two office blocks across the compound to the sun-licked, white-wave-topped sea. A cargo vessel, with containers stacked on its deck, was making its way westwards, moving slowly away from the British coast. Rays of late evening sun caught the vessel, intensifying the bright colours of the containers against the hull and the grey choppiness of the sea.

Gulls on the roof of the office block erupted into their raucous cry, breaking his thoughts. Jack turned to face the room. A puff of cigar smoke billowed either side of his head and he stepped forward, watched closely by the two people sitting in front of his desk. One was Commander Commerford, a sixty-eight-year-old veteran of many MI21 campaigns and activities. The other was Angelica Kane, a thirty-five-year-old expert in undercover work and Field Director within the MI21 team known as 'The Unseen'. Her codename was Angel, partly because she was so good at looking after people. Angelica Kane was neither attractive nor unattractive and was an expert in disguise. She had the sort of face that would blend into a crowd – a necessary requirement for all members of The Unseen. In fact, her only distinguishing feature was a scar on the side of her mouth – gained on a particularly dangerous assignment in Eastern Europe – which she usually covered with carefully applied make-up. Though appearing soft and caring to her enemies, she was as hard as nails and had penetrated several illegal organizations and corrupt foreign governmental departments.

Commander Commerford and Angel studied Jack calmly.

Angel sipped still water from a bottle before she spoke. 'Director, this phone call and all our surveillance information now points to the two children being in direct danger. Surely they should not be allowed to perform their show on Saturday? It's too dangerous. They may not even be alive by then.'

'So you have explained.'

'Jack, we've studied all the data and we know the children are in danger. Immediate danger. Something will happen before Saturday.'

'Yes, Commander, I am aware of this. It is just difficult to comprehend that this is only because they've held on to that disc too successfully.'

'It's not just that, Director,' stated Angel. 'I explained what I saw whilst inside Skunk Headquarters over the last few days. I may only have been his "nurse" but it was obvious from what I heard that Skuda hates those children. They hurt his pride and he blames them for Silas' disrespectful behaviour. He thinks they made a fool of him.'

'He's a ruthless man, Jack,' added Commander Commerford. 'We need to make a decision immediately. We must take action tonight.'

'I know,' answered Jack. 'We've spent the last hour going over all the possible strategies: about what they might do and what we might do. We have two priorities: one is the safety of the children and the other is the hijacking of the Benk ja consignment. There is only one way in which the children can be guaranteed the full protection of MI21, *and* we can capture those Mad Skunks. We must let them hijack the convoy and we have to be lying in wait to take them all. None must escape.'

'In that case, Director, we must go for Option 6, as discussed. Surveillance think they know what the Skunks will do.'

Jack Sanders blamed himself for getting the children into this situation. He had placed them in mortal danger. He hadn't made many mistakes in his life, but thinking it would be fun to encourage his niece and her friend to consider becoming MI21 agents had been one of them. He could understand their parents' fears. However, these would pale in comparison with what was likely to happen over the next few days if the children weren't offered full protection.

The Commander looked at him hard, 'Remember, Jack. When you're in, you're in!'

'When you're in, you're in,' the Director of European Operations repeated.

There was no getting away from it: Mel and Sam were 'in'. They were already seen as agents by an opposing group: the Mad Skunks. When you were 'in' MI21, you were 'in' and there was really no way out; the enemy would always be after you. If the two children were 'in' then they would need to be classed as 'agents' and have the full backing and support of the whole MI21 network. And after all, they had proved themselves to be very useful agents already.

Jack Sanders stood up quickly, the decision had been made. 'OK, we assume it's Option 6 that the

Skunks will go for. We let them hijack the convoy and then we lie in wait for them. There will be a battle, with many casualties, but a huge Skunk unit can be captured. We have to plan for this. We'll meet tomorrow at 0600 hours. And the children are "in". They are now to be fully recognized as field agents within the mighty Ministry of Information for the Twenty-First Century.'

'Good,' said the Commander. 'I'll make immediate plans for the children and their families to be moved to a safe location. As their homes were raided again last night, goodness knows what might happen if we leave them there any longer.'

While the fate of the two children was being decided in a small room in MI21, Sam was hanging by his feet beneath a beam. His arms had been tied behind his back. A chain had been wrapped around his struggling body and padlocked, a gag fastened over his mouth, and a blindfold placed across his eyes. Then his body had been completely covered with a large black sack.

Sam struggled like a maggot in a spider's web. Then he heard Skuda's voice bawling out, breaking the silence.

'And now it's the end for you, Samuel Piper! I've had enough of you and your stupid games. You won't give me the disc, you fruit cake, so I have no alternative but to drop you into the Transforming Hole of Hell. Take him up. We need him to be right over its gaping jaws!'

The rope, over the beam, pulled Sam higher, and a large water container was positioned underneath his wriggling body.

'Now, lower him! Down to where all scumbags deserve to spend their last minutes. Down, down, down! Enjoy your last seconds within the transforming mix of the Hole of Hell. This is the last we will see of the idiotic Samuel Piper!'

Blooming heck, she's good! thought Sam. *She even frightens me!*

On the stage of the village hall, Mrs Eastwood was holding on to the rope which led to a pulley system hanging from the beam. Mel and Sam's parents were helping them put together a brilliant new sketch and they needed a bigger space to practise in. Their rehearsal had been going well, but then, on the spur of the moment, the children decided that the show needed a bit more spice.

Mrs Piper readjusted the huge empty water butt beneath Sam's struggling form while Mel, hidden in the bottom of the container, called out instructions in Skuda's voice. Then Sam was lowered into the butt until he rested on the floor and, hidden from view, Mel helped undo the sack and the rope around his feet. Every so often she called out further instructions.

'Now pour in the bucket of worms!'

Mrs Piper and Mrs Eastwood played out the act with imaginary buckets.

Mel called out a list of unsavoury ingredients: *spiders, head lice, pigs' ears, a ten-year-old collection of nose pickings* . . . and so on. Meanwhile Mel and Sam swapped places.

When Mel was safely tied in the sack, she called out again, 'Up, up . . . Now let us see what transformation has taken place within that dreadful Hole of Hell.'

Mrs Eastwood hauled on the rope and pulled Mel's struggling body out of the container. Mrs Piper pushed the water butt behind the screen and Mrs Eastwood lowered Mel's sack-covered body to the floor. Then Mr Piper, acting as a member of the audience, was asked to help untie Mel.

When she was free she stepped forward towards the edge of the stage. She had drawn a black moustache on her upper lip and cheeks. 'Oh no, look what has happened to me,' she said in Sam's voice. 'I went in normal as Samuel Piper,' then she changed her voice to Skuda's, 'but I've come out as the wicked Mad Skunk Skuda, Master of the Universe. And you are all . . . fruit cakes!'

She was terrific. They all fell about laughing.

'Brilliant,' said Sam's dad from the side of the stage. 'You've got to use that. It's just fantastic! Let's have another run-through after school tomorrow, just to make sure.'

CHAPTER 16

Skunks at the door

Wednesday

AN M121 AGENT SITTING IN AN inconspicuous car watched Mel and Sam sprint out of the gates of Twisted Willow at the end of school. They were keen to get home and practise the new part of their act. Within two minutes Mel's phone rang. It was Uncle Jack. Sam leaned close to hear his words.

'Mel, a quick word. Stay exactly where you are and we will have you picked up. An agent is watching you as we speak. He will take you straight to Apple's house.'

'But we're meeting Sam's dad at the village hall, he'll wonder where we are!'

'Don't worry about that, we'll let your parents know where you are, but it's important you get away, and quickly.'

'Why?'

'Skunk activity. We have information that they are going to strike directly at you. They plan to kidnap you, in order to make you tell them where the original disc is.'

'But how do you know?'

'Our own double agents, Mel. Now stand still and a black Ford will pull alongside. Your driver's name is Harold.'

They turned to see a Ford car moving steadily towards them. Suddenly Sam took the phone from Mel.

'Uncle Jack. It's Sam. Permission to do one small "mission", please.'

'What is it, Sam?'

'If the Skunks are still after the original disc then there has to be something of value on it. We need to find out what that is, but the disc's still hidden. We have to get it out and to safety before they find it.'

There was silence on the other end. Jack was deep in thought. He didn't like to put the children in more danger, but what Sam said made sense, and they were the only ones who knew where the disc was.

'OK, Sam, but when Harold has dropped you off you are to spend no more than three minutes in the house, understood?'

They agreed. The Ford stopped alongside and the driver introduced himself.

* * *

Far away, in the Mad Skunk control centre, the telephone conversation was picked up and relayed to the
correct section. The children now seemed as good as
caught. All Skunks in the Whitewater sector were sent
towards Mel and Sam's homes.

Mel and Sam asked Harold to stop two streets
short of Hillcrest Avenue. Knowing it would be foolish
to walk along the street they headed straight down the
side of a detached house and into its back garden,
quickly climbing the fence. Then they rapidly climbed
two more fences before stopping and leaning against
the one that bordered Melanie's garden. There they
waited a while and regained their breath before peer-
ing over the top. There was no movement in the house,
and no sound from the garden.

Quietly, Sam helped push Mel towards the top of
the fence and then scrambled over himself. They ran to
the back door. Mel took her keys out, praying that her
mother hadn't bolted the door on the inside. She
turned the key silently in the lock, and pushed. The door
swung open. Mel breathed a sigh of relief. But her relief
was short-lived; at that moment the children became
aware of a man running at them from the bottom of
the garden.

They dashed into the kitchen and slammed the
door just as a Skunk agent got the first of his fingers

round the door frame. The attacker howled in pain and Sam realized the door hadn't closed properly. There were four fingers stuck in the jamb. He opened the door a fraction and tried again. The fingers were quickly removed and the door closed, but they could hear a roar of rude words from the Skunk on the other side.

'Quick, Mel, go and get the disc. I'll guard the door!'

Mel ran for the stairs as the agent smashed the kitchen window and glass showered the sink and floor. A hand reached inside; but not for long: it took a direct hit from Sam, who had thrown all his weight behind the frying pan he was holding. A further cry of pain went up. Foolishly the Skunk agent then stuck his head inside to get a better look at his opponent. Sam picked up a bottle of washing-up liquid and squirted it directly into the man's face. The agent reeled in agony, shouting and bawling at the top of his voice.

Gratefully, Sam heard Mel's footsteps thudding towards the top of the stairs. But now the front door was being shoulder-charged. Thinking fast, Sam picked up two bags of flour and ran to the hall just as the door burst open. He launched the bags of flour at the Mad Skunk's face and they exploded in a white cloud, covering the spluttering, choking agent from head to toe. Mel vaulted over the banister and dropped through the powdery haze. Then the two children ran for the back door, Sam grabbing the frying pan as they left.

They flew into the garden and Mel threw herself at the fence. Sam heard the sound of running feet coming down the side of the house. He stepped sideways, the frying pan over his head, and took aim at the first of the two agents pounding towards him. He threw the pan and it twirled through the air, landing right in the agent's chest. He fell painfully to his knees. The second agent, half blind and covered in flour, tripped over him and landed with a crunch on his jaw.

From the top of the fence Mel called out, 'Quickly Sam, there's another one behind!'

Sam took a few steps before launching himself at the fence. He knew that he wouldn't get a second chance; if he failed first time the man would be on him before he could try again.

He didn't. In a second he was over and Mel was leading the escape across her neighbour's garden.

It was then they heard the distant gunshots. Two of them. They looked at each other and picked up speed, heading towards the next fence. They scrambled over it and shot out on to Hillcrest Avenue. Suddenly they heard a man in the street shout behind them, 'There they are!' Mel and Sam's muscles moved into top gear. It was only a few more metres to the safety of Harold's car.

They turned the last corner, but to their leg-faltering disbelief neither Harold nor the black Ford was there. Their eyes ran desperately up and down the road, but their means of escape was nowhere to be seen. Then Sam noticed a small, sunlight-glistening puddle. 'Is that blood?' asked Sam, but before Mel could reply they heard another gunshot. They looked back down the street. Two other Mad Skunk agents were standing in the road behind them. One was crouching, holding a gun. It was pointing at them. To their left they could now hear the thundering feet of more agents. They would soon be surrounded.

'Park. Thirty minutes,' whispered Melanie.

'Park? We should get further out. Perhaps to the farm.'

'Park first. Farm if anything goes wrong.'

'See you in forty-five minutes.'

'Forty-five minutes.'

'Go!'

In that instant they both took off, making for houses on opposite sides of the street. They raced through gardens, zigzagged through streets and over fences, dodging bullets and trying to slow their adult pursuers down. Rule 514: *'When pursued, never stay together if there's more than one enemy agent after you. Never run directly to any safe area.'*

Soon both children were dusty and scraped, their

school uniforms tattered.

After almost forty minutes, Mel made her way to the rear of the small park where they had agreed to meet. Not wanting to use the gate, she climbed over a metal fence well hidden by bushes. Through the undergrowth she could see mothers with their small children in the play area. She watched them for a few seconds. They were no threat. She just wanted Sam to arrive so they could escape to the farm, a deserted complex of buildings where they often went to play.

She was worrying about Harold and what might have happened to him when she noticed a shadow move in the undergrowth, across the grass from where she was hiding. She waited, and saw it move again. Something was definitely in there. She wanted to run, but thought better of it, remembering Rule 525 section 5b in the Agents' Handbook:

'It's not the failure of a hiding place that gives away an agent. It's the movement. Once you are settled, stay still and move only when it is absolutely necessary, even if you are in pain.'

As she watched, the shadow in the undergrowth grew taller: too tall for Sam. It was a man. He stepped sideways and moved towards another bush. A second shadow stood up, stretching its arms. The first passed something to the second. Mel saw a light flicker in the shadows. He was lighting a cigarette.

Mel could do nothing but think of Sam. She had to stop him walking in through that gate. He must not come into the park. She had to warn him.

But she needn't have worried; Sam was already in the park. He was only 20 metres from the children's playground, flat on his stomach, lying on dry leaf-mould beneath an old and twisted rhododendron bush. He couldn't see the danger, but he could feel it. He needed to get out. Something wasn't right here. Time to go!

Both children crept stealthily out of the park, hidden by the shadows of trees and bushes, and melted into the streets again.

Much later, under the shelter of an overgrown tangle of privet and honeysuckle that cascaded over the crumbling wall of the abandoned farmhouse, Mel peeped across the old, disused yard. Where was Sam? She began to wonder whether he had been caught by the two shadows in the undergrowth. Maybe he was trussed up in a room, facing the wrath of Mad Skunk Skuda, at this very moment. Minutes ticked by. She looked at her watch. It was now 5.07 p.m. She had telephoned Uncle Jack on her way to explain why they hadn't reached Apple's. He wasn't available so she had left a message with agent Skydive. Mel had given him the location of the farm where she and Sam planned to meet and Skydive had said he would send someone there to pick them up. Four minutes later Uncle Jack phoned her to remind her not to use the phone when she was in hiding. He was trying to find out what had happened to Harold, but someone would meet them soon.

Movement caught her eye. A crouched shadow alongside the old barn was partially hidden by grasses, weeds and foxgloves. She saw the top of a head and then the curve of a back as it moved forward. It stopped and then darted across a clearing towards the metal railings of the cattle paddock.

The boy-sized shadow was Sam. A smile broke in the corners of her mouth. She watched as he edged his way towards her carrying a plastic bag under his right arm. He came closer and closer until, with a final, scuttling dash, he was over the wall and flat on his back.

'Sam, you frightened me!' Mel lied from the shadows.

He looked over to her. 'No, I didn't. You watched me. I bet you saw my every move!'

'How did you know I was here?'

'Dunno, I just guessed. I saw the wall and the draping foliage and thought, 'That's a good hiding place. I bet that's where she is!' So this is where I decided to start looking for you.'

Mel laughed. 'Why were you so late getting here?

I've been waiting ages.'

'I think I was followed for a while. I had to back-track.'

Mel's eyes were drawn towards the carrier bag, now on the ground. 'And what's that? Have you found something?'

'No,' said Sam sheepishly. 'I've found nothing, Mel. But when we were running around losing those agents I suddenly realized I was near the shop where I . . .'

'Where you what?'

'Where I buy my weekly loaf of bread.'

Mel laughed. 'You didn't! Oh, Sam, you didn't stop to buy a loaf of your bread!

Sam grinned. 'Well, I know it's silly . . . but I wanted it. I'm starving!'

'Oh, Sam!' she giggled. Suddenly she started pulling at the carrier bag. 'Come on then, give it here, I'm starved too! ' She opened the bag and looked inside. 'Oh, great, and you got a drink.'

'A couple of cans and tube of sweets.'

'Brilliant! A picnic!

Soon the children had devoured half of the loaf and the tube of sweets. Never before had so little tasted so good.

They were happily sucking on the last drops in their cans when they heard the sound of an approaching car. They stopped and stared at each other. Melanie peered carefully over the wall. A black Ford pulled to a dusty stop and the driver's door opened. Harold stepped out. He looked a little agitated as he scanned his surroundings. Then, satisfied he was alone, he opened all the car doors and shouted, 'Mel! Sam! I can only wait one minute. Then I have to go. As you can see there is no one else here.'

Sam stood up.

'There you are, Sam. Come on, we've got to go. Is Melanie with you?'

'Yes, she's here.'

'Good,' sighed Harold. 'We must run. We are in great danger.'

Within seconds Mel and Sam were belting up their seat belts as the Ford's tyres spun in a frenzy of spitting dust and grit.

Harold took them further into the country, overtaking a tractor and a van before suddenly turning left on to a bumpy dirt track. The children sat silently, watching him grappling with the wheel as they bounced their way over humpbacks and potholes. All the time he monitored the road behind them in the rear-view mirror.

Suddenly Harold yelled, 'Oh, God, they're here.' His words confirmed the children's worst fears. 'They are only about twenty seconds behind us! The vehicles they've got will catch us in a mile or two. I cannot take you to Apple's. I cannot jeopardize a safe house. They are after me for shooting one of their agents, but I thought I'd lost them. I don't know how they found me out here! If they find you as well it will be a great bonus for them.'

He stopped talking for a moment as the vehicle hit a hump and seemed to fly for a second before smashing into the ground with a twisting crunch. Harold fought with the wheel and managed to prevent the Ford from sliding sideways into a hedge. 'Listen. There's a bend coming up. Hopefully they won't see us stop. As soon as we do, jump out of either side, slam the doors shut and roll down into the ditches. Even if they are full of stinking water you stay there until the Skunks have gone past. Understand?'

'What if there are no ditches?' Sam asked.

'Then climb into the hedges. Just get out of the way, whatever the cost. But do not run down the road. They will see you. When they have gone, phone MI21 immediately and get yourselves back to the farm. Wait there all night if necessary. I will not come back. Somebody else will collect you.'

Almost immediately, Harold swung the car violently into the corner and brought it to a screeching halt.

'Out!' Harold screamed. He looked very frightened.

As soon as the doors slammed shut, the tyres spun, sending flying debris all over the place. The children slid into the ditches on either side of the road. As their heads went down they were aware of the sounds of approaching vehicles becoming louder, replacing the noise of Harold's accelerating Ford.

Sam could feel the bottom of the soft ditch beneath his feet. He fell to his knees and his trousers were soaked instantly.

Mel rolled down the ditch on her side of the road and her legs and stomach sank into deep, freezing water. It took her breath away. She stumbled halfway out, desperate to find an alternative place of safety, slipping and spluttering as splashes of filthy water hit her full in the face. She took out a muddy hand to wipe her eyes clear. The Mad Skunk vehicles were already changing gear and slowing down for the corner; she would have to stay where she was.

But with a jolt Melanie realized that she would be visible to the Skunks as they swung around the bend. The ditch was too shallow to crouch in and as the driver drove round the bend he would be staring straight at her. There was nothing for it but to submerge herself, face and all.

As soon as the first part of the Skunk vehicle came into view, she took a deep breath and dived face down into the water, grabbing hold of grass and weed stalks at the bottom of the ditch to pull herself down out of view.

The driver was gaining on the black Ford in front. He drove faster and faster, keen to catch the MI21 agent and teach him a lesson. Too keen. He misjudged the angle of the corner. It was much sharper than he had anticipated and the back end of his car slipped out of control. The driver spun the wheel to correct the mistake and pressed his accelerator foot to the floor to pull away. But he was too late, the right side of his Lexus jumped the start of the ditch and slammed itself into the hedgerow with a thundering crunch.

Melanie felt the ground and ditchwater vibrate. Pieces of bank and car fell all about her, trapping her legs and knocking the last of the remaining air out of her lungs. The car had crashed and Mel was in desperate trouble.

Sam, oh God, Sam!

CHAPTER 17

Body in the ditch

FROM HER HIDING PLACE, MEL COULD hear the screech of metal and squeal of tyres as the driver of the battered Lexus revved the engine hard in an effort to pull away from the bank. But no matter how much he revved, the wheels spun uselessly in the ditch. The right side of the car was well and truly stuck. Seconds later, the four-wheel-drive Toyota following behind came skidding round the corner and crunched into the rear of the Lexus, edging it closer to Mel's position.

The last of the three cars braked so hard that all its tyres locked on the dusty surface and it spun round and slid into the side of the Toyota. By the time the last car had stopped, the passenger from the Lexus had got out and was shouting instructions to the driver.

'Get this thing turned round and get after that

ruddy Ford. Calypso's gonna pull me out with his tow rope. Do not let that car out of your sight!' With this the man ran quickly alongside the Toyota and the third car turned, wheels spinning angrily, and roared away.

With all the shouting and revving of engines, nobody heard Mel's choking splutter as she brought her face above the water level. Ditchwater exploded from her mouth and nose. She brought up a muddy hand to wipe away the filth from her eyes, but when she opened them it was completely dark. She didn't know what had happened. There were voices all around her. Slowly she realized that the curved front panel of a car was lying over her body, resting on her legs.

Her eyes slowly became accustomed to her dark, watery environment and she turned her head so she could peep from beneath the panel. She could see a man's feet not two metres from her. Now he was crouching down, looking beneath the front of the car.

'Yeah, we can get the rope on here. Move the Toyota round. Let's get going!'

In the ditch on the other side of the road, Sam's heart was in his mouth. He knew he should stay as still as possible, but with two cars crashed right near Mel's hiding place he just had to see what was happening. With his stomach as close to the side of the ditch as possible he angled his head so that only his right eye appeared above the grasses on the road side.

He watched a large Toyota being brought to the front of another car that seemed to have smashed sideways into the bank and ditch.

That's exactly where Melanie is! thought Sam. His heart pounded hard in his chest as he realized that even if she hadn't been injured she was highly likely to be discovered.

With the rope securely attached, the Toyota driver carefully took up the slack and the Lexus driver got back in his car and began to increase the revs. The other man pushed and shouted encouragement.

From underneath the panel, Melanie could see the large four-wheel drive moving away from the ditch, but suddenly the front wheel of the Lexus began to slide closer towards her. She started to panic. Any second now she knew she would have to stand up and run for it, right into the arms of the Skunk agents. There was no chance of escape.

But then, as Mel saw the wheel start to rise up the side of the ditch, she realized that the car was now moving away from her. She held her breath as she watched, convinced it would slide back into the ditch and crush her at any moment. A wheel clipped the panel above her head making it lift for a moment and move away from her legs. Then she heard doors open and men talking as they disconnected the towing rope. She began to breathe once more.

'Come on, let's get going!'

Yes go, pleaded Melanie silently.

She was aware of someone standing on the road behind her. 'What about this wrecked panel?'

'Oh, just leave it! Come on, let's go!'

Yes, leave it!

'No, we can't leave any evidence. You know the boss will go berserk! We certainly don't want Skuda to find out.'

Leave it, leave it! Please, please leave it!

A boot landed on the other side of the ditch. She saw the ends of a man's fingers wrap around the edge of the panel just centimetres from her face.

Oh, God, this is it!

The panel moved and daylight came pouring in around her. She took a deep breath. She'd have to play dead. There was nothing else to do.

Sam watched as one of the men tossed a car panel on to the road. He saw him turn and straddle the ditch. He watched him reach down and pull something up before calling out:

'Goddam it! Look what you've done! You killed a kid!'

Killed a kid! Killed a kid! The words echoed around Sam's brain as he allowed himself to slide down to the bottom of his own ditch. He brought his hands up to his face. *Killed a kid? No, not Mel, no!*

The driver of the Lexus joined the other man and peered down at the body. The first Mad Skunk, clutching hold of the back of Mel's top, lifted her up slightly. She allowed herself to go completely limp and as the water poured off her she took shallow breaths that could not be seen.

'I didn't see her! When I came round that corner I'm sure I didn't see her!'

'I didn't see her either,' said the other man. 'I was trying to make a phone call.'

'What are we going to do with her? I ain't taking a body with us.'

'Chuck her behind the fence.'

'Naw, leave it here. It'll look like she just drowned.'

With this Mel was dropped like a stone face down in the water. She prayed they wouldn't linger longer than her breath could hold.

Then the men had gone, dragging the metal panel behind them.

Within moments Mel could hear shouts, doors closing, and then both cars drove away just as she thought her lungs were about to burst. She lifted her face out of the water and took a glorious gulp of fresh country air.

Sam didn't want to cross the lane. He didn't want to see the lifeless body of his friend or lift her broken corpse out of the ditch and carry it to safety. He didn't want to have to explain to her mother, Uncle Jack and his parents how she had died. But, knowing that he had to do something, he pulled himself out from his hiding place and crossed the road with knees of wobbling jelly.

He saw her legs first. Then her soaking, tattered school top. Then her hair. Then her face. But her dead eyes seemed to be staring straight at him. Suddenly they blinked.

'Hello, Sam. Where've you been?'

With a sharp, jubilant intake of breath he let himself fall forward, rolling into the watery ditch alongside her. 'I thought you were dead, Mel. Dead in a ditch,' squealed Sam, hugging his friend hard.

'So did they! Good acting, eh?'

'They should give you an award for that.'

'Yeah, come on, let's get out of here in case they decide to come back for the body.'

Scrabbling from the ditch, Mel took out her mobile phone. It was drenched. Sam watched her tap a number into it, shake it, then bang it with the heel of her hand. He didn't have to be told it wasn't working.

He walked to the corner of the road where there was a gate into a field. 'Come on. Let's get behind the hedge and decide what to do. It's getting late. We need to get to safety.'

Once out of sight they considered which way they should go. They could follow the lane they had come down with Harold, but they knew they must be prepared to cut across country, avoiding all main roads. Sam worked out they had been travelling east, and he recalled looking at a tree-lined crag of rock set in a long, low hill. If they walked towards the evening sun they would be travelling more or less in the right direction for the farm. As they got closer they would surely recognize places that would help them locate the abandoned farmhouse.

They climbed the gate to commence their journey. Mel glanced for the last time at the ditch that had nearly become her watery grave. The bank had been heavily damaged by the Lexus. There was debris all over the road. Something glinting caught her eye, and, as Sam remembered the half a loaf in his ditch and went to retrieve it, Mel bent down to push aside a tuft of grass. She pulled out a mobile phone. It was still switched on.

She called over to Sam, holding it up. 'Look! One of them must have dropped it. It's working. We'll phone Uncle Jack right now and tell him what we've planned.'

At that moment they heard the sound of an approaching vehicle. Both children scrambled back behind the hedge and lay flat on the ground, fearful that it was the Skunks returning for the phone. It wasn't. The vehicle drove straight past, continuing without a falter. They made the call.

Uncle Jack instructed them to move away from their present location as swiftly as possible. He was sure the Skunk agents would take all possible action to retrieve the mobile phone, especially if it had a store of numbers on it. He told them to turn it off as soon as they had finished speaking, as the Skunks would be able to trace the signal and locate it.

They switched the phone off and headed back the way they'd come. Back to the farm.

The returning Lexus was only fifteen minutes behind them. But when the car arrived at the spot where the 'dead' girl had lain so recently, its driver and passenger were annoyed and perplexed to find neither the phone nor the body anywhere to be seen. In whispers they debated whether or not the police had found the girl and taken the body away. They soon dismissed this possibility. If the police had been called the road would have been closed for investigation. No, someone had the body and that someone probably also had their phone.

After a thorough search of the area they discovered wet footprints in the shadow of the trees. It looked as if they were looking for two people and they were headed back up the lane.

Mel and Sam moved across the fields, frequently stopping, waiting and watching before they moved on. They carefully observed their surroundings; taking everything in; laying a false trail to lose any pursuers. They were good at it. Very good.

The agents in the Lexus thought they had seen them just once, beneath a distant wall. Yet when the car stopped the two crouching figures were gone. At that point the trail, if ever there was one, had evaporated like the wet footprints on the road.

After an hour, Mel and Sam began to see landmarks they recognized, and thirty minutes later they climbed over a gate a few metres short of the abandoned farm. The buildings were just up ahead. Mel pulled out the Skunk phone to summon a driver, but Sam put his hand on her arm.

'Stop a minute, Mel. There's something not right here.'

They both looked up the track. Everything looked as it had done just a few hours before.

'What is it?'

'Dunno. Perhaps the sounds are different. I can hear some angry crows. It just doesn't feel right. Let's get out of sight.'

In a moment they were back over the gate, crouching low behind the hedge as they made their way to slightly higher ground where they could lie flat on their stomachs and look down on the farm buildings. They had only been there a few seconds when they noticed part of the rear end of a car sticking out from behind the old milking parlour.

Mel asked if Sam had noticed it earlier, but he said he couldn't recall any vehicles being there.

After four minutes they moved positions to get a better look. Flat on the ground, not caring one bit about the state of their clothes, they crawled along the base of a hedge for a hundred metres. Any further and they would have been out in the open. They settled down to watch. They could see more of the car now. The passenger window seemed to be open and there was an elbow resting on the ledge.

A slight movement caught their eyes. Away to the left, a man ran from one tree to the next. Then he rested what appeared to be a rifle against a trunk and lifted binoculars to his eyes. He seemed to be tracking the line of the hedge they had just crawled along. They laid their heads flat against the ground.

'Perhaps Uncle Jack's already got somebody here to pick us up, Sam.'

'Maybe, but why are they hiding the car around the back?'

'In case any Skunks arrive.'

'But why would *they* come here?'

Mel was about to reply when they heard the sound of a vehicle. They lifted their heads sufficiently to watch. In less than a minute a van drove into the old farmyard. It was a RapidoPost van.

'Oh, crumbs . . . '

A Skunk agent rolled over the wall Mel had hidden behind earlier. He stepped alongside the driver and pointed round the back of the farmhouse. Another figure emerged from the shadows, waving at the driver.

'It's a trap, Sam! They're trying to make us walk into a trap!'

'But how did they know we were coming here? We could have been going anywhere.'

'The Skunk's phone! They must have monitored the call.'

'But we only said 'the farm'. We didn't need to say anything about where it was. Our lot already knew.'

'But who knew? Only a few people knew about the farm. Somebody's betrayed us. Somebody in MI21 wants us out of the way.'

'Uncle Jack knew . . . '

'Are you suggesting Uncle Jack is a double agent?'

'Of course not, Mel, but who else knew of the farm?'

'Skydive and Harold . . . '

'Well, Harold risked his life to get us out of the car. They may even have caught up with him . . . '

'Wait a minute! It must be my phone. I used it to give instructions. They *must* have bugged it when they broke into our houses. They might have been listening to everything we said.'

'Come on, let's get far away.'

They crawled slowly on their stomachs and eventually cleared all sight of the farm complex. Then they ran as fast as they could for a quarter of an hour, stopping in an old quarry site to get their breath back. Then they finished off the last of Sam's bread and used the Skunk phone to call Uncle Jack.

Forty minutes later they ran to a Ministry of Information car waiting in a pub car park.

They were tired and exhausted when they arrived at Apple's just after 10.00 p.m. that evening. Inside were their families, along with two MI21 Protection Unit agents who explained to them that their houses would be out of bounds until MI21 had made them secure. Both houses were to have new, reinforced windows and doors fitted, along with top-of-the-range burglar alarms and CCTV cameras, front and back.

'MI21 will pick up the bill,' said one of the agents, noticing that Mel's mum looked rather worried. The Director of European Operations was hoping to talk to you about it tomorrow, but I can tell you that MI21 only gives this sort of protection to its agents and their families.'

'But, we're not proper agents . . . '

'Well, as of this week, you are!'

'What?'

'Uncle Jack himself has given permission for both of you to be declared active field agents.'

Mel and Sam looked at each other and then started dancing around and screeching.

Mrs Piper put her hands to her head. This hadn't been a very good week, and the last thing she wanted was for her son to become a fully fledged MI21 agent.

CHAPTER 18

Led into a trap!

AT 11.15 ON THURSDAY MORNING, THE children had to say farewell to Apple and her country cottage with its orchard, chickens and goats. They had barely had time to see the animals, but they had been allowed to rest and sleep late, and they were given a delicious breakfast of eggs freshly collected from the hens, before they left.

The adults seemed to have been discussing quite a lot while Mel and Sam were asleep. But when breakfast was over they were all informed that MI21 had decided to move both families to a new location by lunchtime. Too many people and too much activity at Apple's would attract attention.

They were also told that MI21 agents had taken possession of their homes during the night. It would

take a couple of days to examine thoroughly every centimetre of the properties and their contents, but a few
personal possessions would be checked for bugs and
taken to the temporary accommodation that afternoon. It would be a week before they would be able to
return home.

As they left, they all thanked Apple for putting
them up for the night. They got into two cars and left
separately. When they reached the main road their drivers took different directions to a village called
Nearham, just eight miles from Whitewater.

Eventually they drove through the gates of a large
country house, which sat in the centre of a secluded
garden. The grand building had been divided into eight
apartments. MI21 owned two of them.

The Eastwoods' apartment was on the left-hand
side, on the ground floor, while the Pipers' was on the
right, on the first floor. The children were taken inside
to look round. Each apartment was identical. Both of
them had three bedrooms, two of them en suite, a
large kitchen and dining area, and a balcony overlook-
ing the gardens. Both apartments were fully equipped
with everything they could need, right down to the cut-
lery in the kitchen drawer.

The children were completely taken aback.

'Wow!' exclaimed Mel. 'This is just like a hotel. It's
brilliant! How long can we stay here?'

The excited children explored each other's apartments and then sat down in the Pipers' kitchen to a lunch of shop-bought sandwiches. When they'd finished eating, one of the agents carried in a cat box. The man was wearing shoulder-high leather gauntlets and looked a little shaken.

'This furry fellow caused us quite a problem,' he explained. 'Two of the removal team had to go off for skin repairs! This cat should be working for one of MI21's defence units.'

Everyone laughed, as Puffin hissed and clawed at the metal grille.

'I'll let him out in the other room, shall I?' asked the agent nervously. Sam thought that was a great idea. He didn't want to be the one to open the box!

The children were allowed outside to explore the garden while two agents lingered protectively in the distance. Both Mel and Sam knew they were armed and on the lookout for any Skunk attack.

At 2.00 p.m. two vehicles drove through the gates. Uncle Jack got out of the first car and the children ran to greet him. Men unloaded boxes from a van and Jack explained that MI21 were providing computers so that the children could continue their work on the disc. That was what was in the boxes: a new computer each for Mel and Sam!

The boxes were carried inside, but Jack kept Mel

and Sam in the garden. He needed to talk to them.

'You have a Skunk phone.' They nodded their agreement. 'And it has a collection of numbers on it.' Again they agreed. 'Good, we will need to take it away to study it, but before that we want you to do something for us. We want you to phone one or two of those numbers in an effort to find out what exactly is on the original disc. They have a copy. Try to find out why the original is so important.'

'But how will we do that?'

'Your power of impersonation, Mel. Use your knowledge of known Mad Skunk voices and fool the Skunk agents on the other end of the line into thinking you are someone else.'

'But I only know Skuda' and Claudette's voices!'

'Why don't you speak to one agent, and then see if you can copy that voice when you phone someone else?'

'But we can't do that here. They might be able to track down our location.'

'We've thought of that. We are going to drop you off at a hotel in Whitewater, The Red Lion. They have small conference rooms we can use. Skydive's already there making sure the building is safe. You won't be able to stay long. Thirty minutes maximum, then we'll get you out.'

Ten minutes later they were on their way to the

hotel. Uncle Jack and another agent, Sonia, went with them. When they arrived outside, they were reassured to see agent Skydive there to meet them. He greeted the children and took them inside. Sonia stayed on guard in the reception area while Skydive led them to a room at the back. Inside was a long table and sufficient chairs for ten people.

'OK,' he said. 'I'm going to leave you alone. You can turn the phone on now. I will return in thirty minutes. We are right outside. There's water and lemonade on the table, should you want it.'

With this he left. They turned the phone on and slowly went through the whole list of names. They didn't recognize any of them.

They decided to take pot luck and went through the numbers again, trying to agree on what to say, even though they didn't know what the owner of the phone's voice was really like. Mel was trying to recall the voices she'd heard around her when she was lying terrified in the ditch, when suddenly the phone rang. Mel dropped it in shock and it bounced and clattered on the surface of the table. The children looked at each other, then Mel grabbed the phone. On the display she could see that the caller was someone called 'Sprout-man'.

She deepened her voice. 'Hi, there. How ya doin?'

'Greytooth, where you been all morning?'

'Looking for my phone. Found it in a ditch.'

'You all right? You sound funny.'

'Yeah, I think the phone's got water in it!'

Mel kept the conversation going for a minute and then she asked if they had tracked down the disc yet. Sproutman told her that MI21 had taken over both houses during the night but that he didn't think the Skunk units had found it.

'What do you think was on it?'

'Not my job, Greytooth. Nor yours. We just do what we have to do. Though I know Earthwire was interested. He wanted to know why he was risking his life for the original disc when they already had a copy. Anyway, you delivered that package yet?'

Mel assumed that this was the reason for Sproutman's call.

'No, not yet . . . I've been searching for this stupid phone.' This was the first reply that Mel could think of.

'Well, get it sorted or we'll all be in trouble!'

It was clear the conversation had finished so Mel ended the call. Then she scrolled through the names entered in the phone until she came to Earthwire's number. Mel phoned it without hesitation. A man answered within seconds.

'Morning, Greytooth.'

On the spur of the moment Mel decided to change tactics and voices. 'This is not Greytooth. This is Skuda,' she said, hoping the junior agent would hand over all the information he had to his leader.

'Skuda?' Earthwire had never spoken directly to him before. 'Nice to talk to you, sir, but why are you using Greytooth's phone?'

Mel thought on her feet. 'We're checking all phones to see if any have been bugged. Doing yours tomorrow. We think there's been a leak in project surveillance and we want to know how far information has travelled.'

'Oh, yes sir. How can I help?'

'The disc those fruit-cake kids have. What have you heard about it? I want to know if the truth has been leaked.'

'Well, sir, I am only going on hearsay, but I've been told ... '

'By whom?'

'Steam Train. He said that there was a digital microdot on the surface of the disc.'

'Yes, yes, and what have you heard about it, this microdot?'

'It has to go in some machine or there will a massive explosion.'

'Has Steam Train been told *where* that will happen?'

'I'm sorry, I don't know that, sir. I just know that if the disc is not inserted into this machine, everything will be blown into a billion pieces!'

'Thank you. You've been most helpful, Agent Earthwire. It's clear there's definitely been a leak.'

Mel looked at Sam. Now they knew what to do with the disc, but not where to insert it. They didn't even know what was going to explode.

They stopped talking; they could hear noises and shouts outside. Then came the distinctive sound of gunshots. The children looked around desperately for a means of escape, but there wasn't one. They were in a windowless room with only one door.

A second later three armed Skunks charged in. They were trapped. There was nowhere to run to and the Skunk troopers were upon them. Soon they were face down on the carpeted floor. Sam could see one of the troopers place his gun against a chair while he pulled out a coil of rope. Another produced a roll of sticky tape.

No, please, thought Sam. *I hate sticky tape. I can't get out of it!*

Someone must have heard Sam's plea for at that moment the agent holding the tape suddenly threw it aside, cursing because he couldn't find the end quickly enough. So they were tied up with rope: hands, feet, legs and torso, and the men left the room to bring round a truck.

The moment he saw the last boot go through the

door Sam began to find a way of loosening the ropes. Thirty seconds later he was free and helping Mel to undo her own knots. Together they peeped round the partially opened door. They knew three Skunks had entered, but they didn't know how many were outside. The children looked around the room to see what they could use to distract the approaching agents. There was nothing other than the water and lemonade bottles, plus some glasses and the phone.

Then they heard footsteps and voices heading their way. One said something about remembering the phone. The only thing the children could think to do was to juggle.

When the three Skunks entered the room, they halted in amazement, entranced as water bottles, glasses, a lemonade bottle and a precious Skunk phone flew through the air between the two children.

One of the agents broke the trance. 'Oi, what do you think you are doing?'

This was the appropriate cue for the children to change their aim and fire the glasses and bottles directly at the three troopers. Glass, water and lemonade exploded all about them. Each man took a direct hit and staggered to the floor.

Mel was impressed with Sam's aim. 'Have you been practising? You should be in a show!'

With the door temporarily clear the children made

for the gap. Mel grabbed a piece of rope from the floor and pulled the door behind her. Then she quickly formed a noose and slipped it over the handle, before slamming it shut. She ran forward and passed the other end of the rope quickly over a stair banister, pulling it tight, and Sam tied it off with a knot and two half hitches before they ran to the front of the hotel. Behind them they heard the Skunks shouting and hammering on the door.

As they passed through the reception area they could see Sonia unconscious on the floor to their right and Skydive sprawled on the carpet to their left. But what they didn't see was Skydive's bright hard eyes follow them as they ran out through the front door.

He lay still. He had no intention of jeopardizing his position as a double agent. The children must never suspect that he worked for the Mad Skunk organization. It was, after all, he who had planned to get the children here. His only regret was that he had not arranged for a larger Skunk unit to be involved. Still, five highly trained troopers should have been more than enough for two kids!

As Mel and Sam crept out of the front door they could see a large Mad Skunk on the top step, his back to them, keeping a lookout.

'Knees!' shouted Sam.

Instantly Mel karate kicked the back of the Skunk's

right knee as Sam took the left one. The fifteen-stone, muscle-bound, gun-wielding trooper, collapsed to the floor.

Then, 'Market! Split!' shouted Mel as she saw a Skunk step out of a vehicle, dropping to one knee to aim his pistol at them, and in seconds they were out of range.

Through streets and lanes they raced on their long and indirect route to the market. Forty minutes later, when they were absolutely sure there were no Skunks around, they made brief contact with MI21 and then left for a rendezvous with their friendly Ministry driver outside a bookshop.

During a debriefing session back at their apartments in Nearham it was obvious that Uncle Jack was desperate to know how the Skunks had located Mel and Sam so quickly. Jack admitted that he was concerned about inside information being leaked to the Skunks through a double agent. He explained that they had tried many ways to find out who the traitor was, but the trail always fizzled out, just when he thought they were getting close.

Mel and Sam's parents were told nothing about the afternoon's close shave, though they were informed that the children had been clever enough to find out a little more about the disc, and Jack asked if the children could spend at least an hour before they went to bed exploring its contents. So, after dinner, the children settled down in front of the new computer set up in Sam's apartment.

They checked each file. They had seen everything before. There was nothing new. They went through the Internet connections again, trying to find new website leads, but there were none to be found. Then they took out the disc and examined the holographic square with a microscope Uncle Jack had lent them. Right in the centre of the square was a circle, about 1.5 mm in diameter. This was the microdot, but there was nothing they could do to read any of the information on it.

At 10.00 p.m. Sam's mum announced that it was time for bed. With a 'goodnight' Sam watched Mel return to her own apartment. Half an hour later Sam was in bed and, struggling to keep his eyes open, he turned off the light and immediately fell asleep.

Despite his tiredness Sam's mind was very active that night. At 3.10 a.m. he woke from a dream in which he was reliving that afternoon's close encounters with the Mad Skunk agents.

At 5.20 a.m. he woke again. This time his subconscious had thrown a very important thought into his lake of dreams. Over and over it went in his mind. His eyes were now wide open.

The blank file. The fifteen pages of nothing. No print.

Not a word. Of course there has to be something on there. The text is not in black, though. It must be in white. White on white! Nobody will see it!

In a moment he was up, switching on the computer, and within a few minutes the blank file was before him. He clicked 'Select All' and asked the computer to change the text colour to black. But there was still nothing there. He couldn't believe it! He clicked page after page. Nothing. Not a word. Page 1 – nothing. Page 2 – nothing. Page 3 – nothing. He felt so frustrated; something had to be there. Then, just as he was about to reach the bottom of the document, there it was. Right at the bottom of page 15. Sam's mouth dropped open in shock. So he had been right after all.

It said:

```
           Benk 32 Consignment
    In the event of failure of the hijacking of
the said consignment Agent SD will telephone
Skunk Headquarters. From the control centre a
signal will be relayed back to the convoy. Once
deployed there will be a two-minute countdown,
giving time for any surviving Skunk agents to
make their escape. When the two minutes are up
explosives will detonate, obliterating the
entire convoy and its contents, along with most
of MI21.
```

In the event of a change of circumstances, or to override accidental deployment of the destruct signal, the disc BD3 must be inserted in the master unit within the truck 54TN. The code 5498 must then be tapped into the master unit's keypad. The massive explosive devices will then be rendered useless.

SD

From the clouds to the ground with none but the air to stop him.

Sam pulled the disc out. There, next to the microdot, were the letters BD3. Now he knew everything. If MI21 successfully stopped the hijacking, the Skunks would blow up everything. They had planted massive explosives on each of the trucks. And if he and Mel didn't stop them they would destroy that valuable consignment and many people would lose their lives.

Within a minute he was hammering on Mel's apartment door. At just after 5.50 a.m. somebody within the Ministry of Information got word to a very sleepy Jack Sanders. But they were too late. The convoy had just left and they could not stop it now. To do so would make the Mad Skunks suspicious and they would still blow up the lot.

'There's only one thing to be done,' said Uncle Jack. 'You have the disc. You know the code and where it has to be inserted. We have to get you to the convoy. I'll send a helicopter to take you there within an hour. One of our best agents will come with you. Have some breakfast and dress appropriately. See you soon . . . Oh . . . and well done!'

CHAPTER 19

Stowaway

ON THE MORNING OF FRIDAY JUNE 11TH, at exactly 5.45 p.m., the Benk 32 convoy had rolled out through the impenetrable gates of its south Kent compound. It was right on time.

Despite discussions about the need for extra security the convoy had been allowed to leave as planned, so as not to alert the Mad Skunk organization. Ministry of Information experts believed that somewhere close, at least one Skunk Shadow would be lurking and radioing back information about what he could see. And along the route at least twenty other Shadows would be hiding, probably at major motorway points, making sure that no alterations were made to the anticipated route.

'Operation Flowerpot' was the code word for this

attack on the convoy. MI21 had worked out the likeliest point at which the Mad Skunks would draw the convoy off the road. Through endless hours of research they had analysed the data on the single-page website that Sam had found. From this they had initially pinpointed eight locations where the convoy could be diverted. All of these had been assessed, using long-distance surveillance and even satellite images. Agents on the ground had observed preparations for the hijacking and distribution of the loot. This would be a large operation and MI21 expected the Mad Skunks to use at least twenty-five of their own vehicles including several RapidoPost delivery vans.

Within twenty-four hours agents had narrowed the final destination of the hijacked convoy to three locations. MI21 agents had witnessed suspicious activity in all of them. Then, merely twelve hours ago, Three Cs, Captain Carl Crimson, had had a breakthrough. He discovered that a picture on the website was an encoded map. Now he was sure that the convoy would be diverted off the motorway at Junction 37 on the M1. Three Cs was pretty positive the Skunks would stage a crash, blocking up the carriageway. All traffic would be moved off the motorway including the Benk 32 convoy, which would have priority owing to the value of the consignment.

Three C's had worked out that, once off the motorway, a Skunk unit in full authentic police gear would then lead the convoy in a westerly direction. Another roadblock and diversion would be set up and the Skunk 'Police' would then lead the Benk 32 consignment directly to storage facilities on a large farm. Finally, the roads behind would be blocked by Skunk police cars, at which point the hijack of the vehicles would begin. Three Cs explained that the farmhouse site was ideal. It was hidden away in a small valley, with a wood on one side to absorb the sound of any fighting.

MI21 agents had already been sent to the location. There were thirty 'Leaves and Grass' agents waiting on the ground, hidden amongst the vegetation. Apart from the wood itself, the countryside was very open. It was a difficult area to hide in: but they were there, waiting and observing. Motionless they watched the comings and goings of the Skunk agents, and avoided the half-hourly Skunk patrols. As far as the Skunks were concerned the whole site was secure. They had no idea that their every move was being watched by MI21.

The Skunks also had agents scattered along the edges of the road leading to the farm complex. Some of these were Shadows, trained in the art of camou flage and surveillance, who disappeared from view when vehicles approached. But in the time they had been there, the only vehicles to be seen in the area had been Skunk vans. As far as the Shadows were concerned their cover was secure and the area was safe as houses.

Unbeknown to the Mad Skunks, the Leaves and Grass unit had taken photographs of the Shadows and relayed them back to MI21 Headquarters for identification. And although the unit knew it would soon be outnumbered by the steadily increasing number of Skunk agents, it had been reassured that there were three MI21 troop-carrying helicopters on standby, waiting to follow the convoy on its journey and join forces with the Leaves and Grass unit at the farm.

On the morning of June 11th, Dan Doody was driving the second truck of the Benk 32 convoy as arranged. Dan could see the police escort out in front, and as he looked in the wing mirror of his Renault he watched the rear police car follow the convoy on to the motorway slip road.

Dan was fully aware of the dangers he faced. He knew that the convoy would be attacked in a hijacking attempt and that this was the most dangerous mission he had ever been on. But he had still chosen to do it. He had still signed the form declaring that he was a willing party in this operation. He knew he might never return to Kent, but if he did he would return home a rich man. He had said nothing to his wife about the convoy for she would never have let him go, and for this he felt more than a little guilty. Asleep and content, she had barely stirred when he got up at 4.15 a.m.

Dan sighed as he remembered his silent goodbye to his eleven-year-old daughter. There had been no sound from Emma, just the heap of a duvet covering her sleeping form in the middle of the bed. He wanted to go over and kiss her on the cheek, but he was afraid to wake her, especially as the previous night she had tried to persuade Dan to take her with him on this journey.

Emma loved going away, watching the countryside pass from the cab of her dad's truck. She had wanted to escape school for the day. To see Yorkshire and beyond. To be with her dad.

It was at 7.10 a.m., while Mel and Sam were enjoying an exciting ride across the countryside in a MI21 helicopter, that the sound of a stifled sneeze erupted in Dan's cab. Then it came again: muffled, yet unmistakable. Dan's foot went to the brake, and the cab swayed as he craned his neck round to see behind him.

Sidney, the moody armed guard in Dan's cab, swivelled himself sideways and was out of his seat in seconds, a finger on the trigger of his SR-25. With his free left hand he reached up and pulled down the partially open upper bunk. He was annoyed with himself. He had noticed coats and sleeping bags stuffed into it when he climbed on board, yet hadn't thought to check them out. The bunk swung down to its resting position and a sleeping bag fell to the floor, followed by the legs of a child. Sidney's hands were on his rifle in a flash as the stowaway collapsed to the floor. Dan, still driving, could only glance over his shoulder.

'Oh, no!' was all he could say.

Sidney reached forward, swinging the person around. It was a girl.

'Do you know this person?' he demanded.

'Yes.'

'Well, who is she and what on earth is she doing on this truck?'

'She's my daughter. I've got no idea what she's doing here!'

'Sure you haven't! You know full well we're on a dangerous mission. We can't have any passengers at any time, and certainly not on this convoy.'

'I didn't know she was there!'

'We'll have to get rid of her. She may jeopardize the whole mission.'

'What do you mean 'get rid of her'?'

'She can't stay here and that's that!'

Sidney turned to the frightened girl, and brought his angry face close to hers. 'Just what do you think you are doing here?'

Emma, wide-eyed and shaking, was beginning to regret hiding herself away for a little adventure. She had no idea her father would be riding with such a ferocious-looking armed guard. She now wished she had stayed at home.

'I'm sorry, Dad. I just wanted a day out from school. I wanted to ride with you up to Yorkshire.'

Sidney turned towards Dan. 'What? You told her you were going to Yorkshire? What are you doing telling her about the mission? How many others have you told?'

'Don't be ridiculous,' countered Dan Doody. 'I haven't told anyone about the mission. I haven't said anything!'

'Then how the heck does she know that you are going north?'

'She's good at guessing! She knew it was going to be a long trip because we started out so early. She knew I was staying overnight and that I wasn't taking my passport. There was a crash on the M1 yesterday afternoon and I may have said that I hoped it would be cleared for today. She just picks up clues.'

Sidney grunted, stared hard at Emma on the floor and then told her she was to pull down the small seat behind her father's, sit on it, and not make a sound.

Sidney then contacted central control. He was whispering, but Dan could still make out a few words.

'... major problem ... stowaway ... yeah, stupid kid ... ten, eleven, twelve ... father's an idiot ... need to dump her ... danger to us and herself ... need help here ... no, no ... blasted idiot ... no ... yeah ... service station ... get rid of her ... meet there ... '

'Sorry, Dad!' whispered Emma nervously.

Dan turned and frowned at her. 'Now we're in a pickle. They'll have to get someone to pick you up at the service station.'

Sidney leaned across and banged his fist on the steering wheel.

'Will you shut up, Doody! How much more are you going to say? Are you going to tell her everything about what is planned today? I thought you were one of MI21's most trusted contract drivers. Surely you know better than to say anything about any mission! She may be bugged. She's not been checked out!'

Dan Doody gripped the wheel tightly. The implication that he wasn't trustworthy enough for MI21 cut deep.

Dan drove in silence, time dragged, and he couldn't help worry about deserting his daughter at the service station, but eventually he accepted the fact that there was nothing else he could do. The convoy pulled into the Topline services where the truck and trailer section had been cordoned off.

The Benk 32 consignment was directed into the midst of a collection of armoured cars, troop carriers and tanks. Two jeeps then moved in to block the entrance after the final police car had passed through the barriers.

The police officers got out of their vehicles and were met by disguised MI21 personnel. Dan watched, waiting for the pointing fingers and for Emma to be carted away for some hidden interrogation. But the finger-pointing didn't come. Two officers came up to the driver's door, but this had been prearranged; Dan had expected it. All drivers were to be guarded on their walk to and from the service station, so that they could use the toilets and have a 45-minute break.

When Dan stepped down from his cab, one of the officers said simply, 'And the girl. Take her with you.'

Dan lifted Emma down, putting her gently on the floor.

'I'm really sorry, Dad,' she said yet again, but he merely grunted and led the way to the services. Inside, their guards stood back while they went to the toilets. When he came out Dan expected to see a couple of officials ready to take Emma away, but still no one had arrived to pick her up. He directed Emma into the restaurant area for breakfast and they went to sit over by a window. Two of the other drivers were already eating. He nodded at them. He could see their inquisitive looks. Emma spotted more armed guards around the edges of the room. Most of them were looking out of the windows, ready to protect the drivers from outside threats, but two guards scanned the restaurant, watching the other customers.

Only now could Dan Doody talk freely to his daughter.

'Emma, I don't want to know how you got into the truck, or how you managed to hide for so long. All I know is that we are both in trouble now. I'll be for the chop when I've finished this operation and you'll be carted off any minute.'

'Where will they take me?' asked Emma nervously.

'I haven't got a clue. But you won't be going home until after the mission is over. They seem to think I've disclosed some secret facts to you. So in case you spill the beans you'll be locked up until it's all over. Then they'll take you home to your distraught mother who hasn't got a clue where you are.'

'Can't you ring her?'

'Emma, this is an MI21 mission. I can't ring home. I'm not allowed to. They'd have my guts for garters. I'm in enough trouble as it is.'

'I'm sorry, Dad. I didn't know it was going to be like this. If I had, I would have stayed at home.' Emma's voice wobbled and she cleared her throat. 'What did you mean when you said you'd 'be for the chop' when this is all over?'

'Emma, they won't employ me again. They'll think they can't trust me with a job in case my daughter stows herself on board again. I was to get paid well for this trip. It was going to pay for a surprise holiday for us all.'

Emma burst into tears. 'Dad, I'm so sorry!'

Dan Doody started to feel guilty for making her upset. He put his hand on her arm but she pulled it away. Then they both lifted their heads as they heard a helicopter pass overhead.

Mel looked down below. The helicopter was circling the stationary convoy at a safe distance. The children occupied the only two seats behind the pilot and agent Skydive who had, apparently, volunteered for this dangerous mission. He had listened intently as Sam told him everything about his discovery and the important microdot on the disc.

'You got the disc?' Skydive had asked.

Sam tapped the side of his small backpack. 'Yeah, safely in here. I just hope you manage to find the right vehicle to slot it into in time.'

'Don't worry about that, kid. My instincts will tell me which vehicle's got the timer on,'

Now the children were enjoying the flight with hardly any input from the adults in front. They pointed things out as the countryside flew past. They were excited to see the convoy down below, looking so small.

'Ever fancied skydiving, Sam? It must be great to

fall through the clouds with nothing but the air in your parachute to stop you.'

'I know what's stopping me!'

'What's that?'

'It's called the ground. I don't fancy splatting into it!'

'You'd have the parachute,' Mel laughed.

'Well, it would be great if you knew it was going to work.' Sam paused. 'Wait a minute! What you just said about falling from the clouds, it reminds me of something.' Sam pulled out the code instructions for stopping the countdown. He looked at the bottom line and showed it to Mel.

'Look! *"From the clouds to the ground with none but the air to stop him."* It's about skydiving, Mel. And it's signed "SD".'

'So?'

'SD! Think about it! This message could be from Skydive.'

'Don't be daft,' Mel whispered back. 'He's one of our top agents!'

'I know, but think about it. He's always been about. He was there at that pub; he's the one who knew about us being at the farmhouse!'

Mel looked at the paper again. 'Can't be! He's here to help us. He's going to take the disc and ...'

'Exactly! He's going to take the disc! We are

trapped here with him, and we have no way of stopping him. I bet he's the double agent! And he has no intention of stopping any explosion. He just wants the disc off us!'

'Well, what can we do?'

Sam pointed to the side where a few DVDs were stored for the pilot to play films for his bored passengers. Mel nodded. 'It's worth a try!'

CHAPTER 20

Hijack

DAN DOODY ATE SOME OF HIS BREAKFAST before speaking again. He tried to be as natural as possible, and talk about what he had seen on his last journey: smart trucks; an accident; cows running across a field; the cost of a new tyre. All the small things that he knew Emma liked to hear about.

Eventually she dried her tears, had a drink of freshly squeezed orange juice and ate some of her bacon and eggs.

'When do you think they'll come for me?' she asked at last.

Dan looked around. 'Any minute now, Emma. They are probably waiting till we go back to the trucks.'

As he spoke two of the other drivers stood up. One of them pointed to his watch, indicating it was time to leave.

Dan finished eating and scrunched up his serviette.

'Time to go, Emma.'

'I don't want to go, Dad.'

'You can't stay. It's too dangerous.'

'What do you mean?'

'I can't tell you, sweetheart.' He stood up. 'Come on. Let's go and find the officials who'll look after you.'

Emma stood up reluctantly and walked towards the guards who were waiting to escort them back to the truck.

As they stepped through the doors Dan looked around for the officials. No one came forward.

'Where are they, Dad?'

'I don't know, Emma. Perhaps they're by the truck.'

But they weren't. Emma's heart skipped a beat as she realized there was no one waiting to take her away. Perhaps there was just a chance she would ride with her father up to Yorkshire after all!

As they came alongside the Renault's cab, Sidney moved around the front.

'Climb inside,' said Sidney.

'What, both of us?'

'Both of you.'

Emma smiled at her father, weak with relief. But Dan seemed to have gone deathly pale.

'She needs to get to safety,' he said anxiously.

Sidney shook his head. 'Inside, it's time to go.'

Dan heard the other trucks starting up. The leading police car moved off, followed closely by the Scania, then a gap in the encircling troop vehicles opened up to allow the trucks to move on their way.

Soon the convoy was accelerating along the slip road to rejoin the motorway, making a date with fate beyond Junction 37.

Fifteen minutes went by before Sidney told them why Emma was still in the vehicle. 'The service station was very busy and we know that Mad Skunk agents would have been watching. They knew it was our rest area and so they would have made sure agents were there to look for anything out of the ordinary. If a girl got out of a cab with her father but didn't go back into it, they might have come to the conclusion that we knew she was in danger because of the planned hijacking. That's why she has to stay. Besides, MI21 believe that having the girl on board will relax the Mad Skunks. They know we would not send her into a dangerous assignment so they'll think we don't know anything about the hijacking.'

'Hijacking?' asked Emma. 'What's he talking about, Dad?'

'Just be careful what you say, Doody,' advised Sidney.

'We're on a very dangerous mission, Emma. I would

give anything for you not to be here. It's very difficult to explain but MI21 know that this convoy is going to be hijacked.'

'Hijacked? Do you mean robbed?'

'Sort of, but it's more complicated than that. They're going to try and steal the whole convoy.'

'Well, why are we still going then, if you know? Why don't we just turn round and go back?'

'Because we want them to do it.'

'Want them to? You want them to steal everything?'

'We want them to try. Then they're in for a shock! We are out to capture a large number of criminals and smash a massive section of their organization.'

Emma's eyes were drawn to the heavily armed passenger in the cab. She looked at his finger just millimetres from the trigger.

'Dad, will there be shooting?'

Dan Doody looked across the cab. His eyes met Sidney's and he gave the slightest of nods.

'Emma, this is going to be very dangerous and you must obey every instruction without question.'

'But will there be shooting?' she repeated.

'Yes, Emma. There may be.'

Emma crouched back in her seat. Her mind was jumping all over the place. She imagined windows shattering, shouts of alarm, armed men, and bullets flying everywhere. She sat on the seat behind her father and said nothing, though she wanted to ask how long it would be until they got to where the hijacking would take place. Eventually her eyes returned to Sidney's finger on the trigger of his gun and she hoped beyond hope that her father would be safe in whatever was about to happen.

After a while, Emma fell into a deep sleep. Getting up so early, hiding herself in the back of her father's car, crawling out in the depot when no one was looking and sneaking into her father's truck had taken its toll. She was exhausted, and it was over an hour before she woke up again. She looked around the cab with bleary eyes and there was Sidney sitting in exactly the same position as he had been when she dropped off.

Dan Doody meanwhile had been anxiously looking at the junction numbers. His heart faltered. They had reached Junction 33 already; they were nearly there. He must have been insane to agree to take on this operation. What had he been thinking of?

A few minutes later the convoy reached Junction 34 and a clamminess spread over his arms and neck. For the first time he hoped the hijack attempt would not take place. It was too dangerous, and his daughter's life, as well as his own, was in peril.

As the Benk 32 consignment passed Junction 35, a well-hidden Skunk Shadow phoned Headquarters to let them know the convoy was just passing and that everything seemed clear. This was also confirmed by the Skunk unit travelling in a white van about half a mile behind the last police car in the convoy.

A Skunk unit started up a Volvo truck. It had 'broken down' on a side road just short of the M1's Junction 36 slip road. It had its own 'police' escort of two cars. To all passers-by the police officers had appeared to be questioning the driver while the truck stood on the side of the road. Now the two cars followed it on to the motorway just three miles ahead of the Benk 32 convoy. Within four minutes the Volvo's police escort moved into the two lanes parallel with the truck, so that nothing could pass them. Then, as Junction 37 approached, the Volvo and the police cars slowed to a virtual stop in the slow and middle lanes, and waved traffic past them into the fast lane.

As soon as they passed the slip road to Junction 37 the articulated Volvo swerved violently and came to a stop diagonally across the whole motorway. The M1 was blocked.

Dan Doody could see brake lights coming on up ahead as cars slowed down. In the distance they could make out the blue flashing lights of several police vehicles.

'Here we go,' Sidney muttered grimly, before talking quietly into his microphone.

The convoy started to slow down. Several cars had drawn to a halt behind the rear Skunk 'police' vehicle and soon the convoy was also forced to a stop. Skunk 'officers' got out of their car and ran back to the real police escort vehicle to tell them to get the convoy on to the hard shoulder and off the motorway as soon as possible. The officers were to follow a police vehicle that was waiting at the top of the exit slip road. This would take them on a 'helpful' diversion.

From the moment a Skunk agent had phoned to confirm the convoy was about to leave Junction 37, an increasing number of Skunk vehicles had moved closer to the farm. Some entered the compound, others pulled in to two fields just a mile away. It was clear to the expertly hidden Leaves and Grass unit that the diversion had been successful. The additional Skunks had been brought in to transfer the consignment crates and packages. Everything would be quickly taken off the five convoy trucks and transferred to smaller vans and wagons. These would then be driven away in a variety of directions to several different destinations.

A hidden MI21 agent on higher ground, picking out the approaching convoy, relayed the information to the others. Everything was now set, and at a radius of ten miles away, out of earshot, three MI21 troop helicopters circled the farm waiting for the word. Mel and Sam were on a smaller one, out of sight of the convoy.

The farm location was just what Dan Doody had been told to expect. As they approached he could not see another house anywhere. The Skunks had chosen well. It was totally isolated.

The front police car led them down the drive. The stone farmhouse looked small compared to the metal outbuildings. Beyond the house Dan could see the wood. If things got really dangerous he had been advised to run in that direction for cover.

The Scania in front pulled into the yard. Dan stopped behind it.

'Is this it, Dad?'

'On the floor now, Emma. Lie down and curl up as small as you can.'

Dan looked back to see the other trucks in a line behind him. He was aware of men emerging from the farm and outbuildings. They all had guns. In the mirror he could see the Skunk 'police' hauling the real escort officers out of their cars and throwing them to the floor. A hooded man with a machine gun stood over them in a threatening manner. Dan hoped desperately that he wouldn't fire.

From her curled-up position Emma watched Sidney slide his automatic rifle to the floor for later, dropping a jacket on top, and then pull up another gun.

Dan took a deep breath as he watched two armed men approach his cab. He didn't see the two gunmen on Sidney's side. Other armed Mad Skunk agents stood against the buildings while Blast Troopers crouched or lay guarding the scene, guns at the ready.

Dan's door was pulled open.

'Get down, please sir, and turn off the engine.'

'What's happening?'

'Just get down, please, sir; all will be revealed in a minute.'

Dan dropped to the ground. The muzzle of a gun caught his shoulder as one of the men climbed on board. He soon found Emma on the floor.

'Come on, lass, out you get.'

Sidney wasn't treated quite so politely. A Skunk pulled him violently from his seat, and he landed heavily on the ground outside. The gun he held was wrenched from his hands and thrown some distance away. Then a trooper ran forward to collect it, throwing it through an open doorway into an outbuilding.

A Skunk in combat gear stepped forward with a megaphone. 'Gentlemen, if you have any further weapons you must throw them down. This is a hijack and the contents of these trucks now belong to us.'

This was all the Leaves and Grass unit wanted to hear. The sound of a single shot echoed around the buildings and Megaphone Man spun sideways, clutching at his upper arm. All the Mad Skunks dropped to the floor, scanning the moor for the sniper. Suddenly another shot rang out and a Blast Trooper fell to the floor. The battle had begun.

Dan quickly pushed Emma back into the cab as the sound of shooting increased. They could hear shouts, shots and the sound of bullets raining down on the metal sheets of the outbuildings. Within moments they were both on the floor. Then the passenger door opened and Sidney reached in for the rifle hidden under his jacket.

Outside the Skunk agents fired blindly as the number of shots coming from hidden gunmen somewhere out on the moor increased. Meanwhile, heavily armoured MI21 troops suddenly dropped down from the back of the hijacked trucks where they had been hiding for the entire journey. Before the Skunks knew what was happening they were being shot at from within the farm compound as well as from the moor.

All around the lorry Emma could hear shouts, running feet and the sound of gunfire. But then she heard something that filled her with even more dread.

'Get the girl! They won't shoot us if we've got the girl!'

She turned to her father and gasped. He was almost unconscious, clutching his arm, a spreading red patch on his sleeve showing where a bullet had hit him.

The door swung open and Emma was dragged from the cab kicking and screaming. Her assailant held her in front of him like a shield and backed away towards the farmhouse. Now she could see MI21 agents running across the moorland, firing as they went. Other people made their way behind the buildings. She could see some running into the woods. She didn't have any idea who were the baddies and who were the goodies.

There was a command from the side. 'Stand where you are. Let her go!' She moved her eyes to the left and saw two troopers with rifles pointed directly at her captor. To her right another trooper had his rifle to the Skunk's head. The Skunk realized he was heavily out-numbered and released her instantly. Emma fell to the floor in a heap and scrambled her way back to her father, past Sidney's body sprawled motionless under-neath the shattered cab.

As the Leaves and Grass unit began to secure the area, the three helicopters landed within half a mile of the farm, at three different points. Fifteen heavily armed troopers emerged from each helicopter and spread out in a line to form a defensive barrier through which no Mad Skunk could escape.

Mel and Sam's pilot heard the 'Act Quickly' order and manoeuvred their helicopter to the edge of the farm. Even over the sound of the rotor blades gunshots could be heard. Mel and Sam looked down upon what seemed like hundreds of armed men; some running, others crouching or lying to fire. Some fallen in wounded, sprawling heaps.

Skydive was in an agitated state as he held on to his earpiece. He was shouting into a microphone. 'What? You need to see this. I can't believe it. This is a set-up. It looks like a disaster down there. The enemy's everywhere. They're even pouring out of the convoy trucks. Our men are being cornered like rats. Yes . . . Yes . . . Destroy it! Destroy the convoy! Code Blood Red! Mission failed! Don't worry. I have the disc. Nothing can stop the explosion!

Beyond the main RapidoPost depot, deep within the Mad Skunk Headquarters, Skuda thumped a desk in angry frustration. Then, without hesitating, he gave the signal to destroy the convoy. A technician clicked a cursor on his computer. A box came up: Are You Sure You Want To Destroy The Entire Benk 32 Convoy? The technician looked at Skuda who nodded reluctantly. Far away, hidden on one of the trucks, a timing device began its fateful countdown.

Back in the helicopter Skydive pulled out a gun and twisted in his seat to face the kids. 'Now give me the disc and you'll live!'

Mel and Sam just stared at him, open-mouthed. Skydive then pointed his gun at the pilot. 'Fly higher!

Get us out of here! Whether I have the disc or the kids makes no difference. If it's in here then we are about to see the greatest explosion since St Helens blew up!'

'No! Don't listen to him! We must get this disc to some agents on the ground. It's the only way to stop the bomb!' pleaded Sam, waving a disc case in the air so the pilot could see it.

Skydive's hand suddenly shot out, grasped the case and twisted it from Sam's grip. 'Ah-a! Now I have it and no one's going to use it!' He held it above his head and shot at it. Within the roar of the gunshot explosion Mel and Sam saw the DVD disc and case shatter into a thousand pieces.

'What have you done, you madman!' screamed the pilot as the helicopter lurched to one side. They all looked up at the hole in the cabin roof and then at a shattered piece of rotor blade as it spun past the window.

The pilot fought with the controls, but the helicopter was going down and beginning to spin. The pilot turned to Mel and Sam. 'It's going to be a crash landing. The moment the rotor blades stop you must run like blazes in case this thing blows up. Now open up the doors and get ready.'

Within seconds they all jerked sideways as the helicopter crunched into the field behind the farmhouse. Skydive struggled to release his seat harness, then turned round to point his revolver at the young agents. But it was too late. They had vanished.

Mel and Sam ran through Skunks and MI21 personnel desperately searching for a vehicle with the reference figure 54TN. They had no idea where to look. It might be written on a cab, trailer or wheel arch.

'Thank goodness Skydive didn't spot that you were holding up the wrong disc!' panted Mel. 'I just hope we get to the bomb in time!'

Seconds were ticking past. Suddenly Sam saw it. It was part of a registration number on a Renault truck, the second one in the convoy.

Skydive had picked up their trail and was hot on their heels. He soon saw them dodging between vehicles and shouted out an order to nearby MI21 troops to have them arrested for their own safety.

Sam rolled under the Renault's trailer with a torch in his hand. Towards the front he found a black box secured to the base. He twisted a knob and a cover dropped down. There before him was the digital countdown, flashing red. One minute and four seconds, three seconds, two . . . In a cold sweat he called out to Mel for the disc. There was no response. Sam looked behind him to see the legs of two MI21 field soldiers who were grappling with her. Quickly, he rolled back out from under the lorry and stood up to face them. Then he heard Skydive give the order for his arrest. Just as he turned to the approaching field soldier to try to explain the danger, a man's gloved hand stifled him from behind.

Skydive could see that there was now no possibility of the children stopping the explosion, but he had to get away himself. He turned and ran along the side of the farmhouse as fast as his legs would take him.

Sam struggled and kicked, throwing his legs up in the air in an effort to escape the clutches of his captor. He caught the man off guard and Sam felt his clasp loosen. He gave a final kick and managed to wrench himself free. Swiftly, he ran towards Mel, still struggling to escape, and wrenched the backpack from her hands.

He dived under the truck, fumbling for the disc and the code. The field soldier was crawling beneath the truck after him. With disc in hand, Sam looked at the countdown. Thirty-six seconds to go. His heart in his mouth he tapped in the code 5498, then inserted the disc. He watched in horror as the countdown continued. Then he realized what he'd done wrong.

'No, no!' he breathed. 'Wrong way round! Disc first!'

He pulled the disc out but was suddenly aware of someone grabbing his foot. He kicked backwards with his free leg and inserted the disc again. The agent now had hold of both his feet. Sam entered '5', then '4'. The man was now pulling at him with all his strength. Sam couldn't get his fingers to the keyboard properly. 'No!

You'll kill us all!' he shouted. 'It's Skydive you want. He's a double agent! Please let me stop this bomb. The whole convoy is about to blow up!'

The trooper tightened his grip. 'Skydive? A double agent? You're having a laugh. Children like you have no business messing about with things they don't understand.'

He hauled Sam out from under the truck and pinned his arms behind his back. Sam was almost crying with frustration. 'It's a bomb, I tell you! I know the code: 5498! You must let me go!' But the agent wouldn't listen and began dragging Sam backwards to the farm building.

At that moment Sam saw a young girl he didn't recognize peer round the back of the truck. He shouted as loudly as he could. 'Under the truck! Look under the truck! Press "9" and "8". Hurry, or it will all blow up! 9 and 8!'

The girl hesitated, then quickly wriggled underneath the truck. She found a panel and saw the flashing red signal. Six seconds, five seconds . . . A bomb! It really was a bomb!

Emma took a deep breath to steady herself. What had the boy said? Was it '9' and then '8' or '8' and then '9'? Emma's fingers hovered over the controls. Which was it?

The red signal flashed. Two seconds . . . It was now

or never. Emma punched first the '9', then the '8', and shut her eyes, waiting for an explosion. None came. She counted up to ten in her head, took a deep breath and looked at the timing device. The countdown had stopped with one second to spare.

Emma felt sick with relief. She crawled out from underneath the truck and sat with her back against one of its wheels; her legs were too wobbly to stand up. Soon she saw the boy running back towards her. He was waving his arms and grinning like a maniac.

Sam flung himself down on the ground. 'Thank God you came along! We'd all be dead now if you hadn't. You saved our lives!'

Emma smiled back at him. 'It was terrible. I couldn't remember which number came first. In the end I just took a chance and shut my eyes!' Emma went quiet at the memory. Then she said, 'I've got to get back to my dad; he's injured. He needs help.'

Emma and Sam climbed up into the cab. Mr Doody was conscious but too weak to move, so Sam ran to fetch help from MI21 while Emma sat with him and told him her amazing story.

Mel and Sam had been released as soon as Sam had told his story to a senior MI21 officer, but Skydive was nowhere to be found. He had run away from the inevitable explosion and was now mixing with MI21 troops on the edge of the battleground. Before he attempted his run for freedom he sent a final message back to Skunk Headquarters. 'Skuda. It was those kids. They had the disc. They stopped the explosion. It's all failed. Get them. Somebody get them!'

Skydive didn't get very far. He hadn't gone more than 100 metres across the fields when a group of Leaves and Grass agents rose up out of the long grass. He was totally surrounded. He dropped the phone and his gun. It was all over.

CHAPTER 21

What a catch!

THAT EVENING THERE WAS CONSIDERABLE celebration in MI21 headquarters. Three Cs was beaming with pride. The operation had been a fantastic success. They had dealt a massive blow to the Mad Skunks. They had deprived them of a huge fund which would have allowed them to expand their empire, and the Skunks had lost a substantial number of highly effective agents.

On top of these successes the Benk 32 consignment was safe. Nothing had been lost, though a few items had been damaged by bullets. However, they hadn't yet got Skuda ...

At 10.10 p.m., just as Mel and Sam's contribution to the events was being discussed at MI21, a meeting of High

Command in room C24 at Skunk Headquarters was coming to an end. It had been a very difficult meeting.

Skuda, now released from the hospital ward, banged the table yet again. 'Ninety-six agents lost! Ninety-six! Never, ever has this organization lost so many people. Not to succeed with the hijack was only a remote possibility. Nothing was expected to go wrong. Nothing! Never in a million years should we have lost more than two agents, but ninety-six! And we didn't get even one case from the convoy, let alone a truck!' Again his fist crashed down on the table. Nobody else dared to speak. They knew it was best to let him rant and rave.

'These kids . . . they're *only* kids for goodness sake! Can *nobody* stop them?'

There was a polite knock at the door.

'Keep out,' yelled Skuda, not wanting any interruptions. But there was another knock, this time louder and more urgent. High Command sat in silence, waiting, with Skuda drumming his agitated fingers on the table.

'All right, all right. Come in if you must, but it better be good!'

A woman walked into the room carrying a file.

'Is this absolutely necessary, Siberia?' snapped Skuda. 'Don't you know that a High Command meeting is never, ever to be interrupted?'

'Yes, Skuda,' replied Siberia, pulling an A4 sheet of paper out from the file, 'but I think you might be interested in this.'

'I doubt it!'

'Ah, but you will. This will bring your blood pressure right up to boiling point,' she gloated.

'What is it?'

'My team was charged with making the initial searches through the children's property. We were told to deal with everything to do with the Piper computer. One of my agents found this.' Siberia passed the sheet to her colleague on her left. He gave it a quick glance before passing it on towards Skuda.

Skuda looked at it briefly. It made no sense to him. 'Well, what is it?' he asked irritably.

'It's a list of ten websites,' explained Siberia as she pulled out two further pages from the file. On one there were two photographs. One showed a dog on an upturned flowerpot. The other, a couple with their arms around each other, standing outside a cottage. There was a fine sunset behind them. The second sheet was a print out from the Sun King "K" range on the Garden Sheds I Love Web page.

Skuda was now even more agitated. 'Are you mad, woman? Why the devil are you showing me this rubbish?'

'These were found next to the boy's computer.'

'So? So? He must be a really sad character to be interested in garden sheds. Is he a child or a man? He sounds more like a grandad!'

Siberia didn't falter; she had nerves of steel. 'What you have there was taken from the disc. They broke through our codes. They found everything on it. Everything. Proof is on the computer. We were able to see where they'd been. Every Web page they visited. And there's this . . . ' A further sheet of paper was pulled from the file.

'What is it?' Silas asked.

'It's the list we produced for the Benk 32 consignment hijack. It too was found in that kid's room. He knew exactly what we were going to do. It was the kids. They knew. They did it, Skuda! They broke the code!'

Now Skuda was on his feet, shaking. He pulled off his sweater as he felt his body temperature reach boiling point. He hurled it into the centre of the tables and then, with arms and face pointed upwards, he roared to the ceiling with a rage that no one had ever seen before. His hand reached for a water jug and in an instant an arc of water flew through the air as he sent the jug spinning towards his computer. Glass and water exploded and the screen toppled backwards, crashing to the floor.

'That's it! That's it! I've had enough! Skydive sent

messages that the kids were at the hijacking and that they had the disc. But this . . . ' He shook the pieces of paper before him. 'This is outrageous! How can a couple of kids do all this? I've had enough. I can take no more. By this time tomorrow I do *not* want them hanging by their toes from the ceiling. I do not want them tortured to screaming point. I do not want them sold to a slime-ball in north Italy for the price of a donkey and a crate of oranges. I want them dead!

'Dead! Dead! Dead! And *nothing* else will do!'

CHAPTER 22

The Show

MEL AND SAM ARRIVED AT RUNDALE HALL at just after 5.00 on Saturday afternoon. There was much to do. They wanted everything in place well before the 7.15 p.m. start.

Rundale Hall was an imposing Victorian building that had been built for a wealthy banker. Now it was a residential home for the elderly and also a community centre. Actors and musicians often performed in the ballroom, which had been kitted out with a proper stage and lights. It was here that the Mel and Sam Spectacular Show was to be held.

The manager, Mrs Dennick, looked a little flustered when Mel and Sam arrived. 'What a day I've had! I expected it to be a normal Saturday but I've had all sorts of people here. People I didn't even know were coming. I've had three teams round from the council. One went all over the house checking for vermin! I ask you! Another group looked at the state of the wheelie bins, and the third was checking that the all the electrical appliances complied with European standards! What nonsense!

'Then I've had the water board round; they've been sending rods up and down the drains, and they've even been crawling around the attic. Then the electricity board came along to check the plugs. They spent ages in the ballroom. It's a mystery to me why they've all come at once!'

Mrs Dennick sighed deeply and looked around. 'Right, well, I mustn't stop you. I bet you've got a lot to do. See you later. You know your way round by now. If you want anything just give me a shout!'

Mel and Sam were pleased to hear Mrs Dennick say that workmen had turned up unexpectedly during the day. Uncle Jack had said they would. He was convinced that the Mad Skunks would try to strike at the children during their show, when they were most vulnerable. His informants had told him that Skuda was determined to take revenge on Mel and Sam; that he was quite mad with rage. So Uncle Jack had laid his own plans. His agents were installing all manner of surveillance equipment, including hidden cameras within the ballroom, in the corridor and reception area, and all over the grounds. These, and several micro-phones, would be connected to a central control moni-toring system up in the attic. Vans would come and go all through the day. And when the last van left there would be twelve fully armed agents hiding within the building and grounds of Rundale Hall.

Everyone to do with the show was told that, apart from their contact agent, Julian Six, they were not to speak to anyone who might be from MI21 in case it made any Skunk observers suspicious. 'Just get on with setting up the show. Leave everything else up to us. We'll have agents everywhere. The Skunks won't have a chance.'

With much of their equipment spread all over the floor Mel and Sam began to assemble the show. The backdrop frame was erected; lights mounted; cables sorted; control panel checked; lights adjusted; sound equipment checked. Gradually the whole stage began to feel really special.

By 6.20 p.m. the set was ready. Mel and Sam went over the order of the programme while their mums went to retrieve the picnic baskets. Within a few min-utes they were all tucking into a most welcome meal.

By 6.40 p.m. Mrs Dennick had sent two of her assistants down to set up the chairs, and at 6.50 p.m. the first members of the audience started to trickle into the hall. At 6.57 p.m. Mrs Dennick had a telephone call from the singer and keyboard player who were the evening's other entertainment.

'Mrs Dennick?'

'Yes?'

'Mrs Dennick, this is Pearly White Hawkins and the Midnight Dazzler.'

'Who? Oh, yes . . . our singer. Not having any trouble getting here, are you, Mr Hawkins? I noticed you haven't set your equipment up yet and the Spectacular Show is due to start in, let's see now, fifteen minutes. You'll have to do it all when Mel and Sam have finished their first half.'

'Mrs Dennick, we can't come.'

'Can't come? What do you mean, you "can't come"?'

'Mrs Dennick, I'm awfully sorry but we're . . . we're caught up in traffic.'

'Caught up in traffic? Well, just get here when you can.'

'Oh, I don't know where we are, Mrs Dennick. It's dark here, and we're a bit tied up.'

Primrose Dennick bent to look out through the window at the glorious sunshine outside. 'Dark?' she asked. 'What part of the country are you in?'

There was no reply. Primrose looked at the phone as it went dead. She could have sworn she had heard a muffled grunt at the end of the line.

And probably she did, for Pearly White Hawkins

and the Midnight Dazzler really were 'stuck in traffic'. They were in the sealed rear of a RapidoPost van. There were no windows, and both of them had been tied up: hands and feet. Pearly White Hawkins had just had the phone snatched away from the side of his face as the Skunk trooper thought he was about to say too much.

They had been kidnapped at about the same time that Mel and Sam were arriving at Rundale Hall. Skunk High Command had wanted them out of the way, so that the evening's performance would be cut short and the children could be dealt with at the earliest possible opportunity.

Suddenly Mrs Dennick became aware of how quickly the hall was filling up and went to find her two assistants to put out some more chairs. When she got into the reception area she could see that Miss Biddle was looking rather harrassed at the small table where she was trying desperately to handle all the ticket sales. Mrs Dennick stared at the door.

Who are all these people? she thought. *I hardly recognize any of them.*

People were actually queuing to get in.

'I'll go and get some help for you, Miss Biddle.'

'Thank you, and have you got any pound coins? Everybody's turning up with notes. Some people have gone in without even bothering to wait for their change.'

'I'll go and see what I can do.'

Mrs Dennick scuttled away, unaware of the reason so many extra 'members of the community' had turned up. MI21's Unseen department had been working all day at their character disguises. They had decided to send in eighteen agents, many of them women and several of them disguised to look thirty, forty or even fifty years older than they actually were.

However, these were not the only disguised agents coming through the door. The Mad Skunks had sent thirty of their own undercover agents to Rundale Hall. Most were men disguised as older women. Some stayed outside but most chose to go in to see Mel and Sam captured.

Agents of both sides poured through the door to purchase tickets from the flustered Miss Biddle, mixing in with genuine audience members. Each side suspected the other would be there so there were many sly, sideways glances into the faces of others. But the disguises were so good that nobody could be totally sure who was and who was not a genuine audience member.

Within the ballroom, the hidden cameras relayed information to the team in the attic. Photographs of everyone who entered the hall were analysed by MI21 computers, and matches were sought from their vast database. Agents waited patiently to find out which of the key Skunk agents were in the building.

Mrs Dennick's two assistants were feeling the pressure as they scuttled around trying to set out more and more chairs. The forty became fifty, then sixty, then seventy. In the kitchen Mrs Sloan and Mrs Barcrumble began to get really concerned about insufficient supplies of tea and biscuits. The extra pressure made their hands shake with nervousness as they set up a huge number of cups for the interval. The sound of cups clattering in saucers could be heard above the general chatter within the hall.

At 7.25 p.m. Mrs Dennick moved to the front, took up the microphone and apologized for the late start. She explained that more people had come than expected. Then she told the audience that Pearly White Hawkins and the Midnight Dazzler were unable to come to the show. A large part of the audience cheered. They had obviously seen the act before.

Eventually, at 7.35 p.m., the lights were lowered and the audience of 112 people settled down, ready for the show to begin. Then, just as Mel's mum started the music to signal the start of the act, the double doors reopened and a nurse pushed in an elderly woman in a wheelchair. She wore a hat at a jaunty angle, heavy make up and a black eyepatch over her left eye.

Make-up or not it only took a couple of minutes for an eagle-eyed agent up in the attic to identify the person being wheeled to the front of the ballroom. Confirmation of the identity soon returned via the Internet.

'Skuda!' said Agent Carr, grinning with satisfaction. 'Well, well, well. What a catch!'

'What on earth is he doing here?' asked a colleague.

'Don't know,' she replied, 'but he must really hate those children to be here in person. Make sure Eagle Eye knows he's here. He will have to be watched at all times. He'll be the greatest threat. Though you wouldn't believe it to look at him. He looks like a cross between Captain Hook and my granny!'

Within the hall, Eagle Eye, the MI21 agent in charge of the operation, pressed his earpiece further in to his ear so that he could hear better. He raised an eyebrow at the news but didn't turn round.

Mel and Sam had spent the last half an hour hidden behind the backdrop for their show. Here they could peep through the material unseen. They had already spotted a few familiar faces. Emma and her dad, his arm in plaster, were sitting expectantly in the middle row. Emma had insisted on coming, and Dan Doody, though he knew of the Mad Skunk threat, kept his worries to himself.

Mel and Sam were pleased to see the audience numbers increasing. They would rather perform to a hundred than to thirty. However, the final few minutes had been quite stressful. Not knowing when or how the agents would strike filled them with dread. 'Remember our signal,' Mel said anxiously. 'If you're in trouble pull one red handkerchief from your sleeve. That way Uncle Jack can send in his agents without the Skunks knowing they're coming.'

Sam nodded grimly. 'I'm not likely to forget!' he muttered.

Then suddenly the music changed and Mel and Sam rushed on to the stage trailing streamers behind them.

Mel plucked six balls from the air and was soon juggling to loud applause. Then it was Sam's turn, balancing on stilts and pulling a stream of paper flowers from his sleeve. Suddenly Mel started to throw beanbags to Sam and they juggled these between them, Sam firm on his stilts. The applause got louder. The performance had started well.

Mel and Sam performed amazing feats – rope tricks, balancing and magic. Sam made dogs and flowers out of long balloons and Melanie popped them with carefully aimed throwing knives that flew like lightning across the stage. The applause rose again in appreciation. Next Sam performed his tricks with interlocking rings, ropes, handkerchiefs and cards.

Eagle Eye, ever watchful, asked the surveillance

team for a progress report. All was quiet in the grounds. There was nothing to report. 'Eagle Eye, they all seem to be enjoying the show. Everyone! Their agents and ours! Skuda's clapping so hard his wig's slipped!' Eagle Eye smiled, but rather half-heartedly. *When would the Skunks strike, and just what would they do?*

Mel and Sam had just begun the final act of the first half when it happened. Mel went to pick up her frisbee from the centre aisle. Suddenly the large hand of an elderly woman gripped Mel's wrist and she felt herself being pulled towards the lady's face. Above the cheering crowd she heard the words, 'That was very good. It's a pity it was your final performance!'

Mel looked into the woman's eyes and immediately recognized her worst enemy. Instantly she flew into a cartwheel, her body twisting swiftly away from Skuda's fierce grip as she saw his other hand reach out to grab her. Then she back-flipped on to the centre of the stage and pulled a red handkerchief from her sleeve with a flourish. The audience applauded, thinking it was all part of the show.

Eagle Eye sent a message to Julian Six. 'This is it. The attack is about to start!'

Mel and Sam ran behind the curtain where Julian crouched. 'Skuda's here,' he confirmed. 'If we can get at him first the battle could be over very quickly. Can you think of any way we can get him on his own?'

Mel and Sam thought for a while, then suddenly Mel said, 'I know, Sam, let's use your dad's new cabinet and invite Skuda up on stage to help with the trick.'

Sam grinned. 'Great idea. I bet Skuda will want to hog the limelight, even in that daft outfit of his! Let's do it!'

In the temporary darkness the audience were getting a little restless. Nothing had happened for almost half a minute. Jeanette put another piece of music on and gave the children the thumbs-up. They hadn't practised the act at all. All they could do was pray it would work. Mel and Sam ran out on stage and struck a pose with Mr Piper's new cabinet between them.

They twirled it around to show all sides. They removed the lid and lowered the panels to the ground, hiding the secret compartment underneath. Sam stood on the base with a flourish. Mel then remade the box and clipped all the sides into position. The front panel went up last. Finally Mel pushed Sam down inside the box, put the lid on and locked it into place.

Mel stepped to the side to receive a bundle of swords from Sam's mother. She placed these on the lid, keeping one in her hand. She then stepped backwards and picked up a coconut from the previous act.

'Ladies and gentlemen, these swords are very dangerous. Observe . . . '

Mel threw the coconut up in the air, took the sword handle in both hands, and in one rapid movement split the coconut in two. Milk exploded around her.

The audience roared its approval. Mel stood in the centre of the stage. 'And now I'm going to do something wicked to my friend!' She moved swiftly to the box, inserted the sword point into a slot and pushed, pretending to struggle when it was halfway through the cabinet. All of a sudden the sword point emerged from the other side. Stifled gasps came from the audience.

Mel picked up another sword and said, 'This is hard work for a small girl like me. I wonder if there's a strong man in the audience who can help me?'

'Female' Skunk hands shot up all over the place.

'Brilliant! They've all forgotten they're supposed to be in disguise,' said Eagle Eye, as he looked at the monitors recording the scene. 'Now we can see who they really are!'

Some Skunk agents were even on their feet shouting, 'Me, me, me! Let me do it!' But they soon became quiet when they heard the unmistakable voice of the person in the wheelchair.

'Sit down, you dogs. There is only person who is going to help this young fruit cake murder her friend – and that's me!'

CHAPTER 23

Captured!

SKUDA STRUGGLED OUT OF HIS CHAIR and up the steps. His grey wig had slipped so that the bun hung over one ear, and his make-up had gone streaky, but he was still a menacing sight. All MI21 agents now had their hands firmly on their weapons.

Skuda stepped towards the cabinet. Mel felt herself shake as she passed him a sword. He threatened her with the point, his evil eyes glinting. 'Don't you come anywhere near me. When I've dealt with your friend, I'll deal with you!' he hissed.

Mel stepped backwards as Skuda located the point in the slot. There was a cheer from half the audience as he drove it home. He took another from the pile and thrust it forcefully into the cabinet. Beads of sweat appeared on Skuda's forehead and he wiped his face with the back of his hand, smudging his make-up even more.

He shouted wildly as he thrust each sword through the box, imagining the metal slicing through Sam's body. But as he raised the last one above his head Skuda grinned at Mel. This time he did not use the guide hole. He drove the sword straight through the box, splintering the wood. Mel screamed. Red liquid was seeping from the box.

Skuda was jubilant. He held up his arms triumphantly. 'One down, dear friends!'

Mel, tears streaming down her face, now stood in the centre of the stage. With furious strength she threw three wooden coconut-shy balls at Skuda just as he turned to face her, reaching for his gun.

The first one struck his shoulder; the next his already broken ribs; and the last solid ball hit him right on the forehead, knocking him backwards, so that he seemed to fly to the side of the stage.

The Skunks were now howling for Mel's blood and the battle began. Mel saw chaos amongst the seats and knew that many innocent members of the audience could be injured. She had to get the agents of both sides out of the ballroom. Skunks were climbing up the stage steps. They were after her. She needed to lead them out.

With a last look at Sam's magic box, Mel gave a

prearranged signal. Jeanette Eastwood pressed a button and immediately two explosions of dry ice obscured the front of the stage. Through the smoke, Mel jumped to the floor and ran for the emergency exit doors.

Enraged, the Skunks followed, with the MI21 agents close behind. In no time at all they began a stampede towards the exit, causing alarm among the real audience members. Most had no idea what was going on. Some thought it was all part of the act; others thought there must be a fire, and soon they too were heading for the doors.

The Skunks chasing Mel were ambushed by MI21 agents outside. When they realized what was happening, some tried to turn back into the ballroom but were forced through the doors by the torrent of people behind them. Shouts and threats could be heard coming from every direction. Then came the first shots. The real grannies screamed, and a couple even fainted. It was pandemonium.

At the back of the stage, trapped by Skuda's final sword, Sam struggled to open the box. He wasn't hurt – the sword had only burst a bag of fake blood they used in the act – but he couldn't get out. Through the air holes he watched in fascination the chaos in the hall, where seemingly nice old grannies were bashing the living daylights out of other nice old grannies.

Suddenly he was aware of a pair of feet outside the box. The feet were clad in the largest court shoes Sam had ever seen, and thick black hairs stuck through the beige nylon tights. Whoever it was was pulling the swords out of the box and sending them clattering across the stage.

Sam struggled out of the false bottom and burst throught the lid of the box. He somersaulted to a crouch, not sure who had let him out. As he looked round he saw Mel rushing towards him. 'Sam! Side-ways!' she screamed, as a sword sliced its way towards his back.

Sam threw himself to the side of the stage and Skuda's sword slashed the floor centimetres from his head. Glancing above him, Sam saw the crazy, dribbling grin and the sword swinging down on him again. He rolled away just in time and heard Skuda curse as the sword splintered the boards.

Sam was now on his feet, goading the Mad Skunk, trying to hold Skuda's attention while Mel ran across the stage to get her lasso rope.

'Come on, Skuda! Come and get me! Let's see what you can really do with that sword.' Sam kept just out of reach, dodging the infuriated Skunk who couldn't move quickly enough to reach him.

'I'm gonna split your head like a coconut!' snarled Skuda, limping after him with the sword.

Sam dodged again, and as the sword hit the floor Mel's lasso dropped over Skuda's head and shoulders. She pulled as tightly as she could, trapping his arms to his sides. 'Help me, Sam!' she gasped. 'He's too strong for me to hold on my own.'

Skuda roared with anger and tried to run forward to catch the children off balance, but in his injured state he didn't have the strength. Suddenly he couldn't pull against them any longer and he found himself staggering backwards towards the illusionist's box, which was standing between him and the children. A second later, Skuda's legs hit the side of the box and he overbalanced and crashed on to his back, legs in the air, right into the opening. As his legs, head and arms sank inside the cabinet, Mel and Sam dashed forward, pushed in his feet, dropped the rope inside and popped on the lid, clipping it closed. Then, in three seconds flat they had tied another rope around the whole unit. Skuda was well and truly captured.

Mel and Sam couldn't believe it! They had caught the worst Skunk of all.

'What a team!' shouted Sam.

'You bet!' whooped Mel.

But the children still had work to do. They left Skuda guarded by an MI21 agent, Mel picked up her Frisbees, and they dashed out of the main doors.

Outside it was bedlam. No one was really sure who

was who. Nobody wanted to shoot their own men, so agents were using flying kicks and rugby tackles in hand-to-hand fighting. Now and again agents would run back into the building to chase through corridors and rooms. They overturned tables, broke chairs and ran back out wielding chair legs as truncheons.

In the midst of the madness a woman caught Melanie's eye. Though disguised as an old lady, Mel could see that she was much younger, and she was very fit, running swiftly towards the house. She watched as the woman suddenly changed direction and kicked out at an MI21 agent who was grappling with a Skunk. Her foot caught him with such force he fell to the floor. Sam rushed over to help him, but Mel was rooted to the spot. She watched as the 'old lady' jumped on the back of another agent, pulling him to the ground. Then it came to her. *That's Claudette!*

Mel took hold of a frisbee, pulled her arm back, then shot it forward, flinging it in a dead straight line. Mel watched as it slammed into Claudette's right temple.

The Skunk agent fell to her knees, clutching her head, then looked round to see where the missile had come from. Her eyes refocused just in time to see another frisbee rapidly spinning her way.

She immediately rolled to one side and saw the frisbee ricochet off the back of a man nearby. He staggered, then turned round angrily and, despite his disguise, Claudette could see it was a Skunk.

'Don't just stand there!' she shouted. 'Get the girl! Quick!'

The agent started to run forward, but Mel's next frisbee got him right on his nose, sending him reeling over the grass, bleeding copiously.

Mel was concentrating so much on the accuracy of this last throw that she failed to notice another Skunk sneaking up behind her. Next minute her arms were pinned to her sides, she was lifted off her feet and carried away from the building towards a waiting car.

Mel cried out loud, but a large hand swiftly covered her mouth and nose. She couldn't breathe!

Mel struggled furiously but she couldn't shake the Skunk off. The hand was still clasped over her mouth and her nose. She began to kick and wriggle, her heart beating wildly. She could hear herself making crying, grunting noises beneath his hand.

Thwack! Mel heard a sharp crack and quite suddenly she was free: rolling on the grass, coughing and spluttering. What had happened? Mel looked round desperately, trying to stagger upright, ready to run if this was a trick.

To her amazement, Mel saw the Skunk on the floor, out cold, and her rescuer was sitting on top of him, tying his hands with a large silk handkerchief.

'Emma!' cried Mel. 'Thank goodness you came. I don't know what he would have done to me.'

Emma smiled shyly. 'It was lucky I saw the chair leg under that bush. Someone must have dropped it. I hit him as hard as I could and he went straight down. We'd better get an M121 agent though. I don't want to be around when he comes to. This knot won't hold for long.'

Mel nodded. 'We need to finish this,' she said firmly. 'Go to reception. Eagle Eye should be there. He'll send help. Oh, and could you pick up the megaphone behind the desk and bring it back here? I've had an idea.'

A minute later Skuda's voice blared out from an unseen location. 'Agents of the Mad Skunk Empire. It is over. It is time to give ourselves up. Let us have no more casualties, then we will survive to fight another day. Throw down your weapons and put your hands in the air. All is lost,' shouted Mel.

And no one heard the roars of frustration coming from within the tightly bound cabinet on the stage.

'No, that's not me! I'm in here! You . . . you . . . idiotic fruit cakes!'

In a short while it was all over. Mad Skunks wandered around with their hands up, wondering why on earth they had been told to surrender when they could still have won the battle and captured the children.

Some were angry with Skuda's decision and a few still managed to escape. But the Battle of Rundale Hall was over and the Mad Skunks had suffered another dreadful day.

The battle's end coincided with the sound of the first police cars arriving at the scene. Members of the local community had been very concerned on witnessing hordes of 'old grannies' fighting in the grounds of their old folks' home and thirty-six people had phoned for the police and ambulance services within minutes of the battle starting.

The next two hours were rather a blur to Mel and Sam. They had to talk to the police, to MI21 agents, even to members of the audience. And then they were reunited with their sobbing parents. All were fortified by numerous cups of tea and biscuits. Finally they had to pack away all the equipment. At last, just after 11.00 p.m., both families, along with Emma and Dan, collapsed on to sofas and chairs in the Eastwood's apartment.

Jack Sanders stepped forward into the middle of the room. 'This has been a great day. A victorious day. Another killer blow delivered to the Mad Skunk Empire. And once again we have Mel and Sam to thank for that!'

He stopped and smiled down at them for a few seconds. Then he nodded in Emma's direction. 'And thanks also to Emma for her prompt and decisive actions. Well done, all of you. You were brave. Very brave.

'We are pleased to report that nobody died in the shootings, though there were a few injuries. Three of our agents suffered bullet wounds to their legs or arms. Eight of theirs suffered injuries: five minor gun-shot wounds, two broken arms and one with a broken nose.'

Mel smiled guiltily.

'However, the main thing is that we captured twenty-six of their agents. Only four are believed to have escaped. What is more, we took a superb prize: the great Skuda himself. What he was doing there is anyone's guess. Yet there he was, and now he is in cus-tody, facing a very long prison sentence, all due to the skills of Mel and Sam. Brilliant stuff!

'We nearly caught another big fish: the mysterious Claudette. We arrested her and handed her over to three police officers. They got her inside their van, yet somehow she managed to charm her way out within five minutes.'

'It's a pity she escaped,' said Sam. 'Never mind, you've got it all on tape, from the filming. She'll be on there. You will be able to analyse all the information from today, won't you?'

'Oh, yes. I'm really pleased we installed those secret

cameras high up in the walls. We have plenty of evidence. It was well worth the effort.'

'I don't mean those. I mean the big television cameras at the back of the ballroom. They videoed everything: the show, the audience, the fighting, the lot.'

'Ah, I don't know about those. We've got a problem there. It seems unbelievable, but we don't know who they were. They're not Skunks, we're sure of that. I've got a team working on it right now. I'll let you know what we find out.'

Uncle Jack put down his pipe and looked round for his coat.

His sister stopped him. 'And so that's it, is it? What about us? What about those Mad Skunks out there. What about school for our children next week? What danger are we in? We need some answers, Jack.'

Jack Sanders turned to face them. 'Very well,' he said, 'this is how I see it right now. I honestly don't think the Mad Skunks are going to bother any of you, not for a while, anyway. They've had their fingers severely burned.

'However, this doesn't mean we'll leave them alone. There are many things happening within their Headquarters that we know very little about, but we will get much more information from our prisoners, and when the time is right, we'll strike!

'Your homes are being made as secure as possible

and there will be agents guarding you for several months. Sometimes you will see them. Other times you won't even know they are there.'

He looked directly at Mel and Sam. 'You two have earned a well-deserved rest. You need time off school to get over the traumas of the last few days. We do not yet know when you will be able to return to Twisted Willow, but it certainly won't be Monday. I suggest that you stay away for at least a week while we check every-thing out at your school. We have to know that things are now safe for your return.'

Jack continued more solemnly, turning towards the adults. 'You will all come under the substantial protec-tion of the MI21 force. Your children have already earned our grateful thanks.'

He moved towards the door. 'I have many things to do and many reports to write about what happened over the last few days. I will see you all later next week.' He almost closed the door but then popped his head back round. 'Remember to keep your tree cuttings watered!' And then he was gone.

Dan and Emma stayed for a little while longer, but the excitement of the day had tired the children out and soon the big yawns and nodding heads signalled it was time for bed.

Before the Doodys left, Mel, Sam and Emma made plans to meet up in the holidays to relive all their adventures. Then, with big hugs and goodbyes, Dan and Emma climbed into their taxi.

Three quarters of an hour later the Pipers and the Eastwoods were all in their own rooms, and one by one the lights were going out. Sam lay on his bed for a while going over and over many of the activities of the day.

He was pleased the new cabinet worked well, though he needed to plan an emergency escape hatch at the back. He didn't fancy the thought of being trapped in there again. He was relieved that the battle had been won and so many Skunks had been captured, and he felt proud that he and Mel were now proper agents. But really he felt utterly exhausted. It seemed that the last couple of weeks had just been one hair-raising adventure after another. He just wanted a few days of doing absolutely nothing.

Mel went to sleep easily, though her active, colour-washed dreams made the night long and restless. But when she did wake up, it would be a new day. A Sunday. And she would do nothing. All day long. And it would be absolutely brilliant!

Had either Sam or Mel managed to keep their eyes open a little longer they might – and only might, for it was very carefully hidden – have seen a tiny light, less than one millimetre in diameter, flash in the dark. That was all that could be seen of a tiny transmitter hidden within the stem of each of Uncle Jack's African tree cuttings, which had carefully been transported to the children's bedrooms. The transmitters observed and analysed. Every seventeen minutes they sent information back to MI21: everything was fine. The children were safe and well. And now they were fast asleep.

Uncle Jack looked at the moon before closing his eyes. The soft music and smooth purr of engine and tyres on the motorway was too pleasant. Dreams of holidays soon wafted into his mind as his driver moved him ever closer to home.

Mad Skunk Skuda could see just a part of that same moon through the small escape-proof window of his cell. He shook his fist and snarled at the four walls that seemed to press in on him.

Reaching down he picked up his shoes and hurled them at the images of two children he had drawn on the wall. The noise caused a shout from the landing outside as other inmates woke up.

Skuda shouted out his curses to them all, before settling down and whispering to himself, 'I need to start making plans. These wretched walls won't keep me here for long. I'll soon be out. And then,' he eyed his two sketches, 'you two will be for it. Your days are numbered!'

He raised his arms above his head before shouting at the top of his voice, 'Get me out of here! Don't you know who I am? I am the Managing Director of RapidoPost: the third greatest delivery service on the planet. I shouldn't be in here! You've got the wrong man!'

Back at Skunk Headquarters, lurking in a secret hide-out, a beautiful woman congratulated herself on her getaway. True, the Skunks had been badly damaged by the MI21 raid, but Skuda had been caught. He was out of the way. There was now a vacancy at the head of the Mad Skunk Empire. Who would fill it?

Claudette smiled to herself, then picked up the phone and started to dial.

'Silas? Here's what we need to do . . .'

A note about the author

DAVE SMITH LIVES IN OSWESTRY, SHROPSHIRE, WHICH is right on the Welsh border. He has spent all of his teaching career in that locality. Since 1996 he has been the headteacher of a delightful small rural school where, he says, the children, staff and parents are just brilliant. The school is full of happy children where learning is great fun.

His wife, Mair, is also a headteacher. Her school is in Wales. Their two schools actually meet on the Welsh border. Dave's is like an outpost of Shropshire, defending England from Welsh invaders. And Mair's an outpost of Powys keeping the English out of her secret Welsh valley.

They have two daughters, Helen and Becky, and a white, polar bear of a retriever called Tipsy Lillie, who doesn't like plastic bags.